Most of the stories
in this book have been taken from
365 Rêves d'Or un Conte Chaque Soir
Other stories and poems by Georgina Adams
and Rosemary Garland

Illustrations by

Kerstin Buisson
Michèle Danon-Marcho
Jean Giannini
Monique Gorde
Valisa

366 Dreamtime Stories

translated by Elizabeth Cooper and John Orpen

Hamlyn

London · New York · Sydney · Toronto

First published 1976 by
The Hamlyn Publishing Group Limited
London · New York · Sydney · Toronto
Astronaut House, Feltham, Middlesex, England
© Litor Publishers Ltd., Brighton
English text and translation © 1976 The Hamlyn Publishing Group Limited

ISBN 0 600 32926 7

Phototypeset by Tradespools Ltd, Frome, Somerset
Printed in Italy

1

The Enchanted Garden

Three little fairies lived in an enchanted garden where they grew wonderful flowers and tamed wild animals.

On the first of January they flew away from the garden to visit all the children in the land and give them New Year greetings. Whenever the fairies came across gloomy children, they just lifted them up and with a flash of their wings, carried the children to their garden.

There, a great white swan beckoned the children to climb on his back and they all went sailing along towards a sunny island where masses of flowers, in a multitude of colours, were growing through a carpet of thick grass.

There was an elephant, too, balancing on a tightrope, holding an umbrella, and a giraffe playing on a swing, and you couldn't fail to hear a big, brown bear tapping away on his drum.

In another corner of the garden, there were monkeys playing in the trees, and they blew kisses to the children as they passed; birds sang and whistled in the children's honour, and all sorts of other animals came running up to wish them all a Happy New Year.

All the children went home afterwards feeling that they had really started the New Year in the right way.

7

2

Misty the Cat Tries to Eat the Moon

It was a freezing winter's night and the little goldfish pond in the garden was frozen over, just like a skating rink.

A great yellow moon was reflected in the icy pond and it looked like a round and juicy honey cake.

'Umm!' purred Misty the cat. He hadn't got a home and was feeling very hungry.

He stepped on to the frozen pond. My! How cold it was to his paws. He mewed in dismay and just couldn't reach the yellow honey cake. Then he realised that his honey cake was only a reflection of the great yellow moon in the sky.

He mewed again in despair, and he mewed so loudly that Francis the gardener woke up from his sleep.

Quickly, he jumped out of bed and hurried to the goldfish pond.

He picked up the cold and hungry cat and took it back home, where he gave it some warm milk.

Misty was very happy now and decided to stay in this friendly man's house. He went to sleep on the gardener's bed, where the blankets were warm and fluffy.

'Prrr! Prrr!' purred Misty in his dreams.

Never again would he sleep out in the cold. Now he'd found a real home.

3

Tally-Ho!

Tally-ho! Tally-ho!
A-hunting we will go.
We'll catch a fox
And put him in a box,
And then we'll let him go.

4

Snow for Lunch

'It's snowing again,' said Sally to her Mother. 'It's much too cold to go out – even Furrkins and Purrkins have come into the kitchen to keep warm.' Furrkins was Sally's pet rabbit and Purrkins was a fluffy, ginger cat.

'Well,' said Sally's Mother, 'you could help me make some snow for lunch!'

'Snow . . . for *lunch*?' puzzled Sally.

'Apple Snow,' explained Mummy. 'Now you peel and chop those apples into a pan while I whisk some egg whites.'

When the apples had been cooked – Sally was very careful when she put the pan on to the hot stove – Mummy mashed them. When they were cool, she added them to the egg whites and mixed them together. Then Sally put the fluffy, snowy mixture into glass dishes.

At lunchtime, Sally said, 'I've made some snow for pudding.'

'Well,' laughed Daddy, 'we had better eat it quickly, before it melts!'

5

Snail Hunting

Peter loved exploring in the garden. One day he found a silvery trail which ran from the garden path to a little crack in the wall.

Peter peered inside and called his Father. 'There's a snail in here.'

Peter's Father explained that snails like damp places and, when the weather is dry, they like to hide under large stones or in long grass or by damp walls.

They found a large stone by the rockery and Peter carefully turned it over. There was one splendid snail there but all they could see was his fine shell.

In a while, the snail began to move and Peter saw how first its head appeared and then its foot. Peter's Father pointed out some slime that was coming out of a hole in the snail's body. 'That's how the snail makes its trail,' he said. 'The slime he leaves behind dries into a silver thread.'

When the snail had moved away, Peter replaced the stone. 'I expect he's off to find some lunch,' said Peter. 'Let's go and find some too – I'm hungry!'

 **6**

 7

The Little Rabbit

The New Doll

A naughty little rabbit ran away one day into the great wild wood.

He leapt and danced about among the reddish fronds of the bracken and played among the piles of fallen leaves. He played hide-and-seek among the bushes with the squirrels and the jays and danced with the little weasels.

At last, the wonderful day ended and the sun began to set.

'Goodbye, we're off home now,' said the squirrels.

But the little rabbit didn't mind. Although he was all alone now, he decided to chase the snowflakes as they fell.

And bit by bit, the snow covered all the forest with a fine white blanket where the little rabbit could see his paw marks stretching away behind him – there was a little mark here, and another one there, lots and lots of them.

Then, night fell, the forest went to sleep, and the little rabbit found a warm hole under a bush and curled up in his brown fur coat.

High up in the sky, the stars winked and twinkled as they moved across the tree tops, and the little rabbit fell fast asleep.

It was freezing outside and Sylvia couldn't go out that day.

She had been given a beautiful doll, with blue eyes, and almost as big as she was.

For weeks now Sylvia had been playing with her new doll, who was called Anna.

But Teddy Bear, sitting in his corner of her room, didn't feel very happy.

One day, Sylvia had been very naughty and Daddy had sent her up to her room.

Forgetting her new friend, Anna the doll, she went straight to her faithful Teddy Bear and held him tightly.

Teddy Bear felt very happy.

9

Tom and the Zebra

Among all the other animals on Tom's farm there lived a big, striped zebra.

Tom and his zebra sometimes went for long journeys into the African bush. They were great friends.

One day, Tom's Father gave his son a lovely little pony. Tom was delighted. But the zebra was very unhappy and he sobbed because Tom had forgotten all about him.

The bull promised the zebra that he knew how to help him.

Tom came along then, on his pony.

The bull put down his head and charged and everybody fell over in a heap.

Tom soon realised that he had not been very kind to his old friend, the zebra.

He went to see him and said he was sorry and the zebra was happy again.

8

Sh! It's a Secret!

'Come over here, Linny,' said her Mother, 'I've got a secret for you.'

'What's a secret?' asked Linny.

'That's something you don't tell to any-one else,' answered Linny's mother.

'Well, then, tell me quickly,' said Linny.

'Very soon, you will have a little sister – or a little brother, Linny.'

'Daddy, I'm going to tell you a secret,' said Linny later.

'What's that, Linny?'

'Pretty soon, I'm going to have a little brother – but you mustn't tell anyone!'

'Grandpa and Grandma, I'm going to tell you a secret!'

'What's it all about, Linny'

'Soon now, I'm going to have a little sister – but you mustn't tell anyone.

'Auntie Virginia, I'm going to tell you a secret!'

'What secret, Linny?'

'Pretty soon, I'm going to have a little sister and a little brother! But you mustn't tell anyone!'

The Grand Prince

There was once a prince who was very rich.

But for all his wealth, he was a lonely young man. Few people chose his company for he was forever boasting of his riches.

One day, as he was riding through a vast pine forest, he met a group of foresters enjoying a picnic. The men, women and children looked so happy that the prince asked if he might join in the fun. At first, the forest folk were afraid to share their humble feast with the grand prince but, he looked so sad, that they readily made him welcome.

After that, the prince often went to the forest to see his new friends. He shared his good fortune with them and all the people of his kingdom, who repaid him with their friendship and loyalty.

11 The Skating Rink

As soon as she awoke, Claudine saw that the big pond was all frozen over.

She hurried to put on her skates and went to the pond.

The ducks all followed her too.

The cat mewed. She would have liked to skate as well, but she didn't like the cold.

So Claudine took the cat into her arms and skated round with her on the pond.

'Here I am,' said piglet, Claudine's special friend, and he tried to skate too.

Over he went on the ice, and everybody laughed.

Putting her cat down, Claudine picked up her little pink piglet and skated round the pond with him in her arms this time.

At twelve o'clock everybody was very hungry and went home for lunch.

12 The Little Pig

The pettitoes are little feet,
And the little feet not big;
Great feet belong to the grunting hog,
And the pettitoes to the little pig.

13

A Splendid Marriage

A very important event was about to take place in Mr Penguin's household – his daughter Hortensia was getting married and he had asked all the gentlemen present at the ceremony to turn up in black tail-coats.

'This type of outfit is very elegant, but where do we get it?' everyone asked.

And everyone dashed along to the local tailor.

'It's very urgent,' they all said to the tailor. 'We must have eighteen tail-coats by first thing tomorrow morning!'

'Quite impossible,' cried the tailor. 'I couldn't get them done in so short a time . . . who could do eighteen outfits by to-morrow morning?'

What dismay this caused! What to do? Hortensia burst into tears and Mr Penguin didn't know what to say to console her.

They called a family council and dis-cussed the matter for hours, but no one could solve the problem.

Then, they heard a burst of laughter from one corner of the room. It was old Granny Penguin.

'Well, now,' she said to them all, 'just go and take a look at yourselves in the mirror and you'll solve the problem – hasn't Mother Nature given us the finest tail-coats in the world?'

Everybody laughed heartily – of course, they already had their wedding outfits.

It was a fine and solemn wedding cere-mony and all the town turned out to admire the penguins' elegant suits.

The next time you go to the zoo look out for those well-dressed penguins!

14
Robin Finds a Present

The woodman's children were going home through the forest, and as they tramped through the snow, all blue in the light of the moon, they sang.

Each one of the children carried a cake and a present for someone at home.

'Well, I haven't got anything to give,' said Robin. 'What shall I do?'

As he felt rather sad, he trailed along at the end of the file. He looked all round him, but there was nothing he could see that looked like a present. Not even a mushroom, and even the blackberries had all gone now. So he just threw snowballs and thought.

His brothers and sisters were already a long way ahead and they called back to him, 'Come on, Robin, hurry up!'

But Robin was having fun throwing snowballs and didn't hurry – then, suddenly he saw something under a pile of leaves. He crept closer and saw a little rabbit. He picked it up and stroked it.

'You are a nice little rabbit,' he whispered, 'and I'll take you home with me.'

Granny was sitting by the fire when she saw Robin come in, glowing from his long run back home, and holding a little rabbit in his arms.

'Look,' he said happily, 'I've brought you a present, Granny!'

As Granny cradled the little rabbit she said, 'This is the nicest present of all.'

15

Dance Little Baby

Dance, little baby, dance up high :
Never mind, baby, mother is by ;
Crow and caper, caper and crow,
There, little baby, there you go ;
Up to the ceiling, down to the ground,
Backwards and forwards, round and round :
Dance, little baby, and mother shall
    sing,
With the merry gay coral, ding, ding-
    a-ding, ding.

16

Mr Crusty

'Who's been throwing out crumbs for the birds?' asked Mother.

'It's an old man called Mr Crusty,' said the children.

One morning, when it was very cold, Joan said, 'There aren't any crumbs this morning. Perhaps old Mr Crusty hasn't woken up yet?'

The children went to his house and called to him.

But he didn't answer. Peter went inside his house. The old man was sitting in his chair.

'You've got a bad cold, Mr Crusty,' said Peter. 'We'll get you something.'

Joan brought some hot soup, Anne some tea and Peter some apple pie.

When the spring came round, the old man was much better and he said to the children, 'You can play in my garden.'

And Mr Crusty and the children became great friends.

Oona and the Silver Bird

Oona lived with her Eskimo parents in the ice and snow of Greenland.

Some days she felt very bored in her igloo without any little friends to play with. But she did have lots of toys and her favourite was her penguin doll.

She played with it for hours on end. And one night, after an especially happy day spent playing with her doll, she had a wonderful dream . . . .

One sunny morning, the penguin doll was waiting for her outside the igloo. He was very excited and led her away from the camp as though to show her the way to something he'd found.

Oona felt very excited too as she followed him, quite forgetting that she had promised her parents that she wouldn't stray far from the igloo.

The penguin doll led her a long way away from the camp and at last they climbed to the top of a bank, where a great white plain stretched away in the distance. In the middle of the plain she saw what looked like a large, silver bird.

There were men all round the big bird. They were from a Polar expedition and were camping on the plain.

When the men saw the little Eskimo girl and the penguin doll, they came over and spoke to them.

'Would you like to see the big bird?' they asked.

'Oh, yes please,' said Oona.

And Oona and the penguin doll had a marvellous time exploring the giant aeroplane.

There were sled dogs inside who tumbled out into the snow, and Oona and the penguin doll had great fun playing with them in and out of the aeroplane, and across the white plain . . . .

'Oona! Oona! It's time to get up!'

Oona smiled sleepily at her penguin doll. And she was sure that he smiled back!

Lucy's Special Supper

It was Mummy's birthday and Lucy and her Father decided to cook her something special for supper.

Mother had to promise not to look in the kitchen until everything was ready.

Lucy peeled lots of big potatoes.

'Good,' said her Daddy. 'We'll have golden fried chips with this lovely fish I have bought.'

Lucy's Daddy fried the fish and chips in the bubbling fat until they were crisp and brown. Then Daddy drained the chips in a wire basket.

'Just sprinkle those chips with some salt, Lucy,' he said. 'Then it will be time to call Mummy in.'

Lucy reached into the cupboard and took a blue pot from the shelves.

'Steady!' cried Daddy.

Too late. Lucy had sprinkled SUGAR all over the chips by mistake.

Then Mummy came into the kitchen. 'Did you say "ready"?' she asked.

Daddy laughed and told her what had happened.

'Well,' said Mummy, 'that's how new dishes are created and Lucy has just invented sugar chips! This is going to be a very special supper indeed.'

Martin the Donkey Pulls the Sled

Once upon a time there was a little russet donkey who had mischievous eyes and long, silky lashes.

He lived in the mountains and every summer he used to jump about in the fields and play with the cows grazing amongst the grass.

But, in winter, it wasn't so good – he had to be cooped up in the old stable and had to watch everyone enjoying themselves in the snow outside.

'It must be such fun,' he sighed, 'playing at sleds.'

One fine day, he had an idea. He managed to chew through the rope round his neck and trotted out of the stable.

Jeannette, the little girl who owned him, had got her big sled out of the house and she had an idea, too.

'Come on, Martin,' she called. And she hitched her donkey to the sled and off they went to the village down the road. The tourists found this very amusing – a donkey pulling a sled.

Jeannette had another idea as the tourists gathered around.

'Ladies and gentlemen,' cried Jeannette, 'come and try a sled ride with us!'

Martin was so happy to be trotting through the snow that he had no trouble in pulling the sled along.

Jeannette and her donkey were such a success that they had to turn people away.

And that's how Martin made a name for himself in the little village where, for many years, he pulled the sled and made lots of children very happy.

20

The Toys Have Supper

One night, while the children were asleep, Rosie the doll leapt from her bed and knocked loudly on the toys' cupboard door.

'Up you get, all of you!' she cried. 'We're going to have supper all together!'

Out came the little wooden soldiers, all in line, with their drums beating and sat down in the dining room, next to the skittles.

Bobby, the teddy bear, ran down to the cellar and got some cream, as well as strawberries and raspberries. Fido, the little mechanical dog, set the table, and the clown helped the three marionettes to their places.

As for Rosie, she was busy in the kitchen.

'Here we are!' she cried. 'Supper is served!'

What a feast they had! They ate, they sang, they danced. Never had the toys had such a banquet.

Suddenly, they heard the first stroke of midnight. At once, they cleared away the plates, swept up the crumbs, put everything back in its place and as the last stroke of midnight sounded they all went back into their cupboard, and Rosie got into her bed.

'What a quiet night,' yawned the children, when they awoke the next morning, for they hadn't heard a thing.

Tina and Tini

Tina and Tini, two young penguins, were having fun sliding down a snow bank.

'These two will drive me quite mad,' said Mummy Penguin, 'sliding and skidding about like that. They'll break their legs if they aren't more careful!'

But Tina and Tini didn't listen. They went faster and faster until suddenly they couldn't stop and – bump! bump! – they fell over each other and tumbled into a hole.

Their cries brought Mummy Penguin running, but there was no real harm done and she soon had them on their feet again.

After this, they promised to be good. They went off to play and built a snow-penguin instead of sliding down snow banks.

21

Prickles, the Hedgehog

'Look, Mummy, I found a little hedgehog half-frozen with cold, on my way from school,' said Peter when he got home.

'We'll put him in a basket by the fire,' said his Mummy.

Poor little hedgehog, he was so cold he couldn't move at all – neither his nose nor even one of his prickles!

Very slowly, warmed by the fire, the little hedgehog moved his nose up and down and then opened his two black and shining eyes to look round him.

He soon lapped up the bowl of warm milk that was put in front of him, and then he set off to look round the big kitchen.

They called him Prickles, and he soon became Peter's firm friend and everyone became used to seeing him shuffling about the house while he waited for the spring.

23

Snow Rabbit's Surprise

One bitterly cold night, great big fluffy snowflakes fell from the sky, until every-thing was covered with a snowy blanket.

Owl watched as the world turned white. He knew every branch and twig for miles around. He saw everything.

Early in the morning, White Rabbit hopped out of his burrow. How different everything looked! Only yesterday he had discovered a field of carrots nearby – and now they had disappeared.

White Rabbit hopped over to Owl's tree. 'Do you know where those carrots are, Owl?' he asked.

'I do, hoo hoo,' chuckled Owl. 'You're *sitting* on them!' And, when White Rabbit cleared a patch of snow, he found as many, long crunchy carrots as he could eat!

24

Hop, Skip and Jump

What fun it is to roll about in the snow, to throw snowballs, and to hop, skip and jump in a soft, white world!

Patrick's cheeks are red in the cold air and streams of frosted air are coming out of his mouth.

Soon it will be time to go in – Patrick is as hungry as a wolf!

The Old Wall

'My goodness, I'm not to be envied,' complained an old wall out in the country. 'In summer, the sun is so hot it cracks my stones. There's not a bit of shade and I feel like an oven. In autumn, things aren't any better. One or two of my stones work loose and when the winds blow, down they fall.

One day, I shall fall to pieces completely. And then there's the rain, which goes right through me, to say nothing of the leaves which blow up against me and stick there, making me shiver all winter.

What an awful season the winter is! The snow gets into the cracks between my old stones and then the ice makes me as hard as – well, stone. I'd die of cold if the thought of spring didn't keep me warm.

Then spring comes and flowers grow all over me and hide the holes that winter's made, and I feel young and carefree again. In fact, I feel as young as the children who scramble all over me in summer.'

26

Pussy

Granny was knitting Grandpa a pair of red woollen socks. She had just reached the toe of Grandpa's left sock, when Pussy pounced.

Four little paws hugged the round, red ball, while Granny looked on in despair. One by one the stitches flew off the needles as Pussy, the wool and Grandpa's sock rolled over and over on the floor.

Now Granny is knitting another pair of socks, in blue wool this time, but Pussy is nowhere to be seen. Granny has put him in the garden until Grandpa's socks are finished!

Timmy and Ricky

It may sound odd, but Timmy, a young dog, had a rabbit for a friend.

Every morning, during the cold weather, Ricky came to play in Timmy's kennel.

But, one day, Ricky didn't come – could something have happened to him?

Timmy decided that he would have to go and see what the matter was, so he trotted off, across the fields all white with snow, to Ricky's hole.

He knocked on the door and a feeble voice answered, 'Come in!'

The little rabbit was not feeling well. Timmy ran off to get the doctor.

'Nothing to worry about,' said the doctor, 'just a cold.'

So Timmy became nurse for a few days and gave Ricky his nose drops and medicine each morning.

What a fine friendship they had!

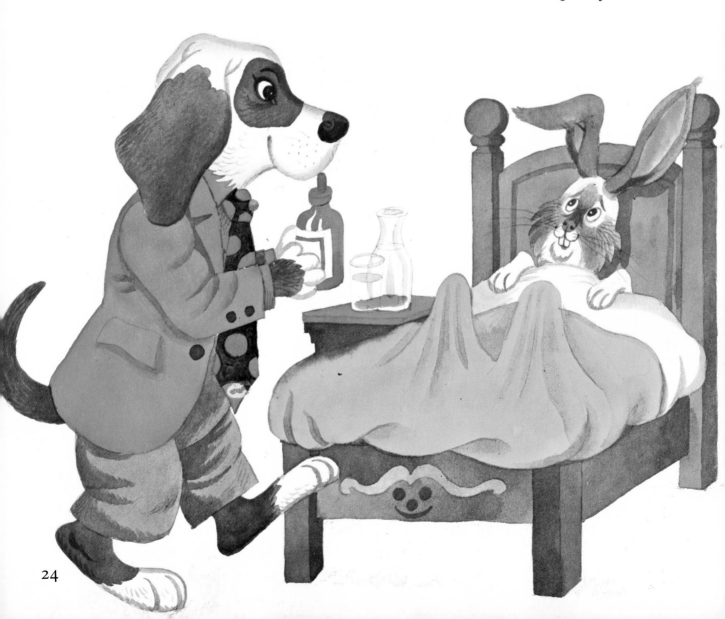

Friendly Encounter

There was a young wolf who had often heard the tale of Little Red Riding Hood, and one day he trotted into the nearest village to make it up with the children who lived there.

Along came a little girl, all dressed in red, with a basket on her arm, heading for the wood.

He came up to her and said, 'Little Red Riding Hood, we've been made into enemies by that old tale about the wolf and Little Red Riding Hood – it's all just a fairy story, you know . . .'

'But children don't believe that any more,' said the little girl.

'Good, then let's be friends,' said the young wolf. And friends they were.

28

Hot Chestnuts!

'Hot chestnuts!' cried the chestnut seller. 'Hot chestnuts!'

The passers-by stopped, bought some and warmed their hands in front of the chestnut seller's brazier.

The chestnuts cracked and popped and split and smelt delicious.

'Hot chestnuts!' cried the chestnut seller. 'Hot chestnuts!'

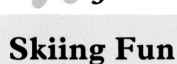 **30**

Skiing Fun

Down the slope, faster and faster!

And then – whoosh! Over she went, face into the snow, and the skis up in the air.

Laura's little friends all burst out laughing.

'Well, go on – it's your turn now!' she cried.

One after another, they lined up and shot down the slope. What fun – even if you do take a tumble now and again!

 **31**

Two Young Squirrels

The forest had donned its white mantle of snow. Everything was quiet and cold.

Only two little squirrels had come out from their nests in the cold weather – they were very hungry.

The summer had gone by all too quickly in playing games and visiting their friends in the wood.

Though Mrs Weasel had warned them that they must lay in a store of food for the long winter – they didn't bother – so what would happen to them now?

The two little squirrels went up to a cottage on the edge of the wood.

'Mummy!' called out Dennis, 'come and see these poor little squirrels lost in the snow!'

'They're shaking with cold and they look starved,' said his Mother. 'Go and bring them in right away and put them down near the fire. We'll give them some nuts to eat, and then we will give them something to get them through the winter for their store cupboards!'

The Two Bears

One day, at a zoo, a little brown bear and a little white bear met and became firm friends.

'One of these days, I shall leave here,' said the little brown bear to his friend.

'And one of these days, I shall leave here as well!' answered the little white bear.

So they both decided the best thing was to escape together from the zoo.

They ran and ran, over streams and through forests, and across fields.

At last they reached a great harbour and without waiting, scrambled aboard a ship.

'Let's hide under these sails,' said the little brown bear.

And then, after a very long voyage, the little white bear and the little brown bear saw the pack ice of the arctic.

Joyfully, they jumped off the ship and ran to make holes in the ice to catch fish.

They had a good meal and then slept peacefully in their warm fur coats.

And that's how a brown bear came to be seen in the arctic.

33

Francis Tells a Story

Francis was a little boy who was always catching colds.

His school friends made fun of him, because he didn't like fighting and games and making a noise.

One year, his class was chosen to go to winter sports and all the other boys were delighted.

But just as soon as Francis put his skis on, he fell over and everybody laughed at him. After trying a few more times, the ski instructor gave him up as a bad job and crossed his name off the list.

The school sent him to an old couple in the mountains and with them he learnt to love the long walks they took there.

Francis learnt all about the animals and plants that he saw and made notes about them in his diary.

When the ski holiday was over, the teacher asked all the children to write down their stories about the holiday. The story Francis told was so well-written that the school's headmaster decided that it should be read in every class in the school.

When Francis saw the admiring looks in his school friends' faces, he knew that they wouldn't make fun of him again.

34

Sally and the Sparrows

One morning, in the snow, the three little sparrows whom Sally had befriended found a young fox, half-frozen with cold and very hungry.

Quickly, they flew back to her house and tapped with their beaks on the window, calling out, 'Cheep, cheep, cheep!'

Sally went to open the window for them and fed them with crumbs and scraps of food.

'What is it?' she asked them. 'Are you cold?'

'Cheep, cheep, cheep!' they answered.

They flew all around her, not bothering about the food for once. It was very odd – usually they were always hungry!

'There must be something they want me to see in the forest,' thought Sally, so she quickly put on her coat, her boots and her gloves and went after them.

'Quick, quick, cheep, cheep, cheep!' they called.

The sparrows flapped their wings, circled round her and seemed to be leading her on into the forest. They even pulled her by the sleeve!

The little girl started to run and was soon out of breath.

And at last she saw the little fox, lying in the snow with its eyes closed.

'Poor little fox,' she said, 'you must come back into the house with us.'

She picked up the little fox and wrapped her arms around him, and for still more warmth, put her long, woollen scarf round him as well.

Then she ran back to the house.

She warmed some milk on the stove and rubbed the little fox with a towel to get him dry. At last, he opened his eyes.

'Humm! It's nice and warm here – and something smells good!' he said.

He drank all the milk and felt much better.

'You must stay with us all winter,' said Sally. 'You'll be well looked after.'

The sparrows finally ate up their crumbs and the scraps, and the little fox curled up on Sally's knees and went to sleep.

'We mustn't wake him up,' said Sally, gently putting the little fox into a warm basket near the fire.

'Thank you, little sparrows, for telling me. You are nice little sparrows. Now we've got a new friend, yours and mine.'

 **35**

The Snowman

'The snow fell all last night,' Mummy said to Jack. 'You can go and build a snowman in the field.'

Jack gathered lots of snow together and built a lovely snowman with a briar pipe in his mouth, two walnut shells for eyes, and a cork nose.

Mossy the dog barked with joy. He leapt all round the snowman and made such a mess that the snowman toppled over.

Jack told him not to be such a silly dog.

'Now come on, help me to rebuild my snowman,' he said to Mossy.

But Mossy found soon enough that the snow was very cold and he didn't want to work so hard.

He ran away towards the house.

Jack felt rather angry, but he got to work and soon rebuilt his snowman. His hands got very cold and his little friends the sparrows came to help him. Then Lisa came out to help also, and when they had finished the snowman looked even better than the first one.

'Come on, Mossy, but this time you sit still!' called Jack.

Mossy came out, and sat quite still near the new snowman. But he couldn't keep absolutely still, so he barked and wagged his tail, while Lisa and Jack danced round the snowman.

The Little Clog

A little clog, all dirty and cracked, was thrown away on a farmyard rubbish tip. All alone in the snow, he felt sad. The pigeons made fun of him, the geese thought he looked awful, the cat sniffed him, and the dog barked at him.

Mary's Mother threw the little clog into the dustbin.

His brother clog was already inside, completely broken up.

Little clog got up out of the dustbin and went sadly off on his own, down the snowy slope.

On his way home from school, a little boy picked him up and brought him back home.

The little boy's house was warm and dry. The children all helped to wash the little clog. Then they painted it blue with pretty red and yellow flowers round the edges.

Then they put a sail up inside and sailed it out into a big pond of clear water.

And so little clog became a little boat which sailed round and round the pond to the joy of the children in his new home.

36

The Cobweb Spinner

Mrs Owl was very proud. She had three lovely owlets with soft, silky feathers and large round eyes. Every evening, she took her children to the tree-top school but her youngest daughter, Hoots, didn't like school at all.

Poor Hoots. Flying lessons terrified her – she hadn't a head for heights and hunting lessons seemed a waste of time, since Mrs Owl always provided them with plenty to eat.

There was one thing, however, that Hoots really enjoyed and that was spinning. Her teacher had bought some silks to teach some spiders how to spin cobwebs and found out that Hoots was good at spinning cobwebs, too.

One day her teacher said, 'Hoots, the schoolroom windows look so bare. Would you like to spin me some cobweb curtains?'

Of course, Hoots was delighted. Now she loves going to school. It's the only one for miles around with cobwebs at the windows made of silk!

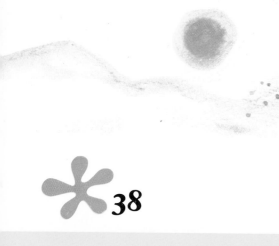

38

The Three Wolves

On a freezing cold night, the Eskimos were at work in their igloos.

Three wolves were prowling round looking for something to eat.

They came up to Yawa, one of the sled dogs, but he was not going to let himself be caught by wolves – hadn't he fought off the Polar bear before now? He ran into the igloo and barked to warn the Eskimos.

The Eskimos laid pieces of bait round the camp and inside the bait they put some sleeping powders. Although the wolves hesitated to eat these tempting pieces of seal they were so hungry that they ate them.

It wasn't long before they all yawned and went to sleep!

The next morning, when they awoke they found that they had been attached to the sleds, along with the other dogs of Yawa's family.

The wolves were very unhappy. They let fall great round tears, which looked like funny rings round their eyes.

But soon the wolves settled down to their new life pulling the sled and after all, it was better to be fed every day than to starve out in the cold.

They soon learned to run with the other dogs and were very happy.

32

39

The Bird Who Brought the Spring

While she was looking through the windows at the clouds hurrying by, Sally saw a bird tumble into her garden. It was very tired and covered in snow. She hurried outside and picked up the little bird. Soon, she had put it down by the fire to warm.

It was a very pretty little bird, but just hadn't any strength left. So she fed it some seeds, gave it a little water and arranged a perch for it to swing on.

Towards evening, the little bird seemed much better; it had eaten all the seeds and settled down for the night on its perch.

The next morning, Sally uttered a cry of joy – the snow had gone from her garden, the trees had all come into flower, and the lawn was covered with daisies and buttercups.

'It's spring!' cried Sally. 'It's come very early this year!'

She ran out into the garden and the little bird followed her. It was quite well now and sang very loudly.

'You're well again,' said Sally to the bird. 'I am glad.'

'Oh, I wasn't ill at all,' replied the bird, 'it was just that I had such a weight on my back – you see, I was carrying the spring!'

Sally clapped her hands for joy. She ran inside to get her dog Popeye and then all three went off into the country to see the spring flowers in the fields. Everywhere, birds were singing and butterflies gliding among the fresh flowers, and there were squirrels leaping about in the long grasses.

When it had seen all it wanted, the little bird said goodbye to Sally.

'Are you going already?' asked Sally.

'Yes, I have to carry the spring to lots of other countries but I shall come back to see you as soon as I have finished my work. Goodbye and thank you.'

He flew straight up into the sky and disappeared into the distance. Popeye barked his goodbyes while Sally waved with her little white handkerchief.

Then she gathered up a great bunch of flowers and took them back to the house.

40

The Colt

Shoe a little horse,
Shoe a little mare,
But let the little colt,
*   go bare, bare, bare.*

41

The Snowdrop

'How hard the earth has become!' sighed a young snowdrop.

And she pushed as hard as she could against the frozen crust of earth which held back her young green shoots. But, despite all she could do, she couldn't get through the earth above her.

'I should so like to see the sky,' sighed the little plant. 'And to sniff the air above and feel the touch of snowflakes on my leaves!'

Pip, a kindly little worm who lived next door, heard her plea.

Taking pity on the little snowdrop, he dug and dug all round the top and finally made a hole in the hard earth so that the snowdrop's leaves could come through.

The little snowdrop thanked Pip. Now she could see the trees and the blue sky and was very happy.

Four

Two's company,
Three's none.
But four will make
Our games more fun.

✳ **42**

Rusty's Surprise

Rusty, the youngest of the squirrels, had 'flu. He had to have lots of hot water bottles and lots of weak tea – he felt rather unhappy stuck in bed.

While his brothers and sisters were all playing in the trees, he had to stay in bed.

'Why should I be the one to catch 'flu?' he groaned.

Mother Squirrel comforted him by saying, 'I've got a surprise for you!'

'What is it?' asked Rusty.

'No, I'm not going to tell you yet, you'll see later on,' answered his Mother.

And off she went into the kitchen for hours.

That evening, when the whole family was sitting round the dinner table, Mother Squirrel brought out a great big almond pie.

Everyone clapped their hands for joy.

'This is a surprise pie,' said Mother Squirrel. 'It's to help Rusty to get well again very soon.'

Rusty tucked in and felt better straight away. What a wonderful Mother he had!

 **44**

The Apple Tart

It was half-term and Caroline had invited her friend, Paula, to stay with her.

Mummy was in the kitchen making an apple tart. 'We are very good cooks,' said Caroline. 'May we help?'

'Of course,' said Mummy. 'Now first put on your aprons and wash your hands.'

Soon the two friends were very busy. Mummy showed Paula how to carefully chop the apples, while Caroline beat two eggs in a basin for the pastry.

When the tart was ready, Mummy put it into a hot oven to bake.

Caroline's Daddy came into the kitchen. 'Mm! something smells good,' he said.

'We've made an apple tart,' said Paula.

'With just a little help from Mummy,' added Caroline.

'Then it should be an extra-specially good apple tart,' laughed Daddy.

And it was.

 **45**

Toothache

Sylvia was in a very bad mood. She had a toothache. One of her little teeth was soon to fall out and was wobbling about.

'Let me have a look at it,' said Mummy.

'No, it might fall out altogether,' cried Sylvia in alarm.

'Well, all right, then we shall have to go to see the dentist and he'll fix it,' said Mummy.

'Oh no, I don't want to see the dentist either,' cried Sylvia.

'Now, really, Sylvia, we must do something with it, and you have to let it come out because there's a new tooth coming up underneath it. I tell you what, tonight you can hide the tooth underneath your pillow for the fairies to find. Tomorrow morning it will have gone and there will be a coin in its place from the fairies.'

'All right then,' said Sylvia, 'let's go to see the dentist so that I can have my old tooth to put under the pillow tonight.'

 **47**

The Grammar Lesson

Jeremy was idly turning over the pages of his grammar book when suddenly all the letters started dancing about – the A began to hop, the S turned somersaults, the O yawned and everything began to go round in circles. Then the chair jumped over the table, the kettle began to sing, the grandfather clock leaned over to speak to the little mantel clock and the grammar book began to juggle with its pages.

Suddenly, Jeremy heard his Father's voice, 'Hallo! the boy's fallen asleep instead of learning his lessons – wake up, Jeremy!'

Startled, Jeremy picked up his grammar book, which had slipped down to the floor, and got down to studying again as quickly as he could.

 **46**

Georgie Porgie

Georgie Porgie, pudding and pie,
Kissed the girls and made them cry;
When the boys came out to play,
Georgie Porgie ran away.

Nicky, the Playful Squirrel

An otter and a squirrel were the best of friends. All through the summer, in and out of bushes and hedgerows, they played hide-and-seek.

But Nicky, the playful little squirrel, always used to win each game because as soon as it seemed he might lose, he would hop straight up a tall tree.

From there, he would lean down and tease his friend the otter.

All too soon, winter came, with snow and rain and cold, and lots of the rivers burst their banks and flooded the fields.

The otter didn't let the cold bother him, his fur was made to keep it out, being all sleek and shiny.

One evening, Nicky the squirrel was right at the top of a tree nibbling nuts when the floodwaters brought the tree crashing down, and into the icy water he fell!

'Help!' cried the little squirrel.

It was just as well that the otter wasn't far away and he dived into the water and pulled his friend out.

'Get on to my back,' said the otter, 'and we'll swim for the bank.'

The squirrel resolved that he wouldn't make fun of his friend the otter ever again, and they remained the best of friends.

49

Silly Billy

Lisa and her three special friends the dog, the farm cat and the billy-goat were playing hunt-the-parcel.

It was Lisa's turn to hide her eyes and count to ten, while her friends looked for a good place to hide the parcel in the woods.

'. . . eight, nine, ten,' counted Lisa slowly. 'Coming!'

She didn't have to look very far. The billy-goat had the parcel stuck between his horns!

'I didn't think you would look for it there,' he laughed. 'What a silly billy I am!'

50

Singing Song

I sing, I sing,
From morn till night,
From cares I'm free,
And my heart is light.

✳ 51

The Wooden Horse

✳ 52

It Is Snowing!

Polly was a wooden horse on a roundabout, but the roundabout was getting old.

Once long ago Polly had a beautiful white coat, big black eyes and a long, long tail. Now all her paint was wearing off, and she wasn't quite so beautiful, but the little children still loved to ride on her back. They would hold on to her mane and gallop round and round to the sound of the music.

One day Polly heard her master say that he was getting too old to run the fair and that he would have to sell the roundabout.

Polly was very sad. She didn't know what would happen to her.

But then she heard him say, 'But I'd never sell old Polly. I'll give her to a little girl or a little boy who hasn't many toys, and who will take great care of her.'

Polly galloped round and round for the last time, but she didn't mind leaving the fair now that she would soon have a new home to go to.

Great, thick flakes of snow were falling steadily all over the countryside and covering everything with a white blanket, so that you couldn't even see the roads.

Nothing stirred!

Except Master Fox, who was on the prowl, shivering with the cold.

Watch out, little chickens, make sure you hide away safely in your coops, because Master Fox is on the prowl!

40

Big Tom

'Now, where has Mousikins got to?' said Mother Mouse anxiously. 'That child makes twice as much trouble as the others. One day, Big Tom will get him and eat him up!'

'I'm here, Mummy,' said a squeaky little voice, and there was Mousikins, hauling a huge piece of cheese along behind him.

Then, suddenly, Big Tom rushed up to them and they got away just in time.

What a lucky escape!

54

Rikki, the Hamster

Rikki the hamster had got so bored one day that he had eaten all the cakes laid out for tea, and scattered the crumbs all over the place.

Then he went and hid himself where no one could find him!

Catherine was very upset.

Hours went by with no sign of the hamster, that greedy little pet.

Catherine began to get worried and called out, 'Rikki, you can come out from your hiding place now – you won't be punished!'

That little hamster was lucky to have such a forgiving mistress as Catherine!

 **55**

Paula and Minnie the Cat

Paula was bored. She had to stay indoors while Mummy went shopping, because it was too cold for Paula to go out with her.

She wandered round the house, from one room to another, but nothing seemed to be of any interest.

Minnie the cat, whom Paula never bothered with very much when she had her own friends into the house, seemed to understand how Paula felt – cats can get bored too!

Minnie scampered up to her, then suddenly turned and vanished and Paula thought, 'I wonder if Minnie wants to play hide-and-seek?'

So they played hide-and-seek and Paula began to feel much less dismal. In fact, she felt very glad of Minnie's company and they played until Mummy came home.

 **56**

Mother Fox

The little rabbit trembled and shook. He was cold and frightened. His parents had been killed by hunters and now he was all alone.

Mother Fox heard the little rabbit's sobs.

'Come and stay with me and my little foxes,' she said. 'You can stay with us until the spring.'

The little rabbit was so glad to be with a family again, and the time passed quickly in laughter and games.

When spring came the little rabbit left, but he promised the little foxes that he would visit them often to play with them.

57. Jacky the Parrot

Jacky the Parrot

Jacky's Grandmother lived all alone. For company, she kept a very fine parrot called Flinders, who talked and chattered all day long and was very good at copying things he heard people say.

Every morning, Jacky passed her Granny's house on the way to school. And every morning Granny would be at the window and call, 'Good morning, Jacky. Have a good day!'

One morning, as Jacky was hurrying by she heard, 'Good morning, Jacky. Have a good day!' But when she looked at the window, Granny wasn't there.

Jacky ran to the front door and opened it. 'Come in,' called a feeble voice from inside the house.

Jacky found her Grandmother sitting up in bed. 'I have a very bad cold today, dear,' she said. 'I have nearly lost my voice.'

'Then who was that calling me?' said Jacky, puzzled.

Granny didn't have to answer.

Flinders was sitting on his perch near the window. 'Good morning, Jacky,' he cried. 'Have a good day!'

'Well done Flinders!' laughed Jacky. 'Now I shall come and visit you every day, Granny, until you are quite better.'

58

Puzzle

My first is half an animal – like a mouse. My second falls from the sky.

My third is part of my leg.

My fourth is what I say when I see my favourite cake!

You will find my whole in the garden!

Solution: *gerbil* – rain – knee – yum! (geranium)

60

The Quarrel

There were once four firm friends : Blackie, the cat, who was completely black, Snowball, the dog, who was completely white, Sunny, the canary, who was a beautiful yellow, and Colette, a very sweet little girl.

One day, by mistake, Snowball upset Blackie's bowl of milk. The cat was most annoyed and scratched the dog. Snowball, who didn't like this at all, fled into the garden, pursued by Blackie, who was followed by Sunny and then by Colette, who was wondering how this quarrel was going to end!

And there they all were, mewing and barking and whistling and running about after each other.

Then, they all began to feel rather tired and everybody stopped the chasing about at the bottom of the garden.

'How silly of us to make such a fuss about a bowl of milk!' said Colette. 'Let's all kiss and make it up.'

And so our four friends forgot their quarrel and went back into the house again to play together.

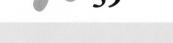

59

The Racehorse

'Come on gallop, big horse! I can see a cloud of mist coming from your nostrils this cold and frosty morning, and your beautiful mane streams in the wind.

Later, when we get back to the stable, I'll give you a rub down and whisper in your ear, because I know you like that.

Then, it will be time for breakfast – a whole bag of oats just for you.

In the spring, on the racecourse, you'll be the fastest horse there is and you'll win every race!'

61

Mrs Marmot and Mrs Mole

After a long and hard winter, nature started to wake up, and the birds cheeped and built their nests. The forest came to life, and the trees started turning green with fresh leaves.

One fine morning, after their long sleep through the winter, Mrs Marmot and Mrs Mole stretched and yawned. The warm sun was enticing them to poke their noses out of their holes.

'My, what fine weather!' said one of them.

'What a beautiful day,' said the other.

They met by chance on the trail into the wood.

'Have you slept well, my dear?' asked one.

'Very well, thank you, but I'm very hungry now.'

And off they went as quickly as they could towards the glade where they knew they'd find all sorts of delicious food; roots, grasses and even a few worms.

But when they got there, imagine their surprise to find the glade occupied by a most peculiar animal who had neither head nor tail.

This was old Mrs Tortoise, who had heard our two friends talking and had hidden in her shell.

'Good-morning, ladies,' said old Mrs Tortoise, popping her head out from her shell. 'Come over here, the grass is delicious.'

Mrs Marmot and Mrs Mole had a splendid feast of grass and roots, but they couldn't find any worms!

They had such a wonderful day together that the three animals agreed to meet again the next day for another delicious lunch!

62

Loopy the Duck

Loopy the duck lived on Maxine's farm with lots of other animals.

One day, despite the sun's rays, he wasn't too keen to slip into the water.

'Quack, quack, that looks very cold to me!'

'Well, if you're not going to take a swim, we'd better go and find something else to do,' said Maxine.

Loopy decided to tease the dog instead, so he bit one of his ears – just gently, of course!

The dog didn't like it at all and chased the duck so hard, Loopy had to jump into Maxine's arms for safety.

She put him down by the garden water tap. The duck thought it would be a good joke if he turned it on – out shot the water, and it rained over everything and everybody in the garden. What a mess!

But Loopy found this all very amusing.

Maxine's Mummy didn't, and she locked Loopy away in the coop.

But later Maxine was allowed to let Loopy out and she led him to the duckpond where he could play with his brothers and sisters again.

63

Forest for Sale

Old Father Michael was selling his part of the forest, and the magpies were all asking each other who would buy it.

'Claudine's Father,' said the flowers – as if they really knew.

But the owl was pleased. He saw Claudine and her Father coming to look at the forest. Claudine was singing.

'We'll build some little place here for our holidays,' said Claudine.

She sat down next to the spring which bubbled out of the ground.

A beaver came up to her and held out his paw as a sign of friendship and a doe took her to meet the rest of the animals.

Claudine knew she was going to be happy in the forest.

64

Pip the Sparrow

In an old drystone wall there were frequently pieces of stone which fell away and left nice round little holes behind.

In one of these Mrs Sparrow was rearing a brood of noisy and hungry little sparrows. One day, one of them fell out of the nest – and it would be the youngest one, too.

The poor little sparrow cheeped loudly in distress. One of his wings was injured. All the while Mrs Sparrow wheeled and flew around, not sure what to do for the best.

On her way back from school, Annette saw Mrs Sparrow fluttering about and went to see what the matter was.

She soon found the little sparrow on the ground and picked it up. She gave it some water and tasty seeds and kept it until it was ready to fly. The wing soon healed completely and Pip, as she called him, flew back home again.

But he wasn't really wild any more and when the spring came round Annette made him fly away to build his own nest like the others. But each day Pip flew back and perched on her shoulder, and thanked her for being so kind to him.

65

In the Barley

Like Emma's eyes,
In the barley
Cornflowers grow.
Like Patrick's cheeks,
In the barley
Poppies glow.

66

The Beautiful Siamese Cat

Cathy was a very pretty little Siamese she-cat who was admired by everyone.

She had a blue bow round her neck and her basket was lined with satin of the same colour. Her mistress, Mrs Joanna, was as proud of her cat as of her antique furniture, her flowers in vases, and her pieces of old china plate.

Recently, she had been awoken by cat-calling outside her windows.

And then all of a sudden, the cat had stopped calling and everything was quiet again.

What a surprise the old lady had in the morning – now there were two cats in the basket! Cathy the Siamese had found a friend – a big, furry cat fast asleep in the basket.

And Mrs Joanna hadn't the heart to chase him away, since Cathy was so happy with her new friend.

67

Monday Alone, Tuesday Together

Monday alone,
Tuesday together,
Wednesday we walk
When it's fine weather,
Thursday we kiss,
Friday we cry,
Saturday's hours
Seem almost to fly.
But of all the days
Of the week we will call
Sunday, the rest day,
The best day of all.

68

The Little Frosted Fir Tree

Out on the pavement, a little fir tree had been thrown away for the dustmen to collect.

It still had its decorations on, too.

'I was so happy in my forest,' it sobbed, and the tears rolled all along its branches.

Two mice came past and asked the tree, 'Why are you crying?'

'I want to go back to my forest,' said the little tree.

'Don't worry – we'll help you.'

The mice got their friends along – two rabbits, a hedgehog and two young foxes.

'Come on, off we go – we'll carry the little tree back to the forest.'

When they got there, they all dug a big hole.

'Make sure you spread my roots out properly,' said the little tree. 'And please could you put a little water on them until the snow falls again?'

They all worked hard and when they had trampled the earth down well, they left the tree who thanked them all very much.

When the spring came, the little tree grew lots of new, green shoots and became one of the finest trees in the forest.

A — As in Africa

One day, Catherine found a big letter 'A' in the garden. She sat on the bar across the letter 'A' – and suddenly she found herself flying up into the sky. She held on tightly to the sides of the 'A' and before long she had landed in Africa!

She was met by a little African boy called Joseph and he took her to see the local market.

They wandered round looking at the brightly-coloured stalls – there were flowers for sale, and funny-looking fruit, as well as curiously-shaped fish. Joseph's Mother gave Catherine a mango to eat.

She went to see their thatched house and they gave her lunch of cuscus and fish.

Then she and Joseph played African musical instruments – the tom-tom was great fun.

The next morning the sky was even bluer and the sun still hotter.

Joseph's Mother went off to the market, where she sold hens' eggs. Catherine had a waffle and some milky coffee for her breakfast.

Then the two children went off to the beach where they found lots of funny-shaped shells.

Finally, Catherine had to say goodbye to her little African friend and she climbed on to the letter 'A' and sat on the bar again.

Away it flew and soon she had landed in her garden.

She had lots of stories to tell her parents about her visit to Africa.

70

The Coloured Clouds

A blackbird was looking at the sky. Against the blue background he could see, here and there, different coloured clouds – there were yellow ones, orange ones and a lot of green ones too.

'It's spring!' called the cuckoo.

The clouds came down on to the land – the yellow ones bore buttercups and yellow marguerites.

The green ones had leaves and grass.

The orange ones carried tulips and other orange flowers.

The little rabbits were very glad to have such tender grass to nibble.

In the woods and fields, along the hedgerows, the children found masses of pretty flowers.

The trees all grew beautiful new leaves.

The little mole was astonished to see such a mass of brightly coloured flowers.

The last cloud to appear among the green ones carried the spring, a little sandy-haired boy with a smile for everyone. He sang all sorts of songs.

The blackbird, the cuckoo, the mole, the girls and boys, picked lots of flowers and they all sang and danced and spring went on its way right across the world.

71

A Wonderful Day

John leapt from his bed and dashed into the kitchen, where he knew his breakfast was waiting for him.

It was going to be a wonderful day!

It was Wednesday and school was closed for half-term.

First of all, he would go and feed the little white rabbits in the hutch, then he would feed the chickens.

But he mustn't forget Zulu, the little foal, or he'd be jealous in the field on his own – even though it was carpeted with daisies!

When John had finished feeding the chickens, he went to play with Zulu. They had lots of fun racing across the field with the lambs.

When it was time for John to go home the little foal trotted back to the fence with him. He had had a wonderful day.

And so had John!

The Enchanted Kingdom

Little grey mouse, the blackbird and Brian all lived in the same house. Brian inside the house, the little grey mouse in the tool shed and the blackbird on a branch of the tree in the garden.

One lovely morning in spring, Brian went to pick violets in the wood, accompanied by his friends little grey mouse and the blackbird.

All the leaves were green at last and so was the fresh grass.

A little ray of sunshine, quite small, suddenly beckoned to them and they all followed him to his kingdom.

It was a very long journey, but when they arrived in the sunshine kingdom, what a sight they saw!

There were flowers, a bit like yellow daisies, but so much bigger than the ones in Brian's garden. And there were great big yellow trees.

And the sun ate only honey and apricot jam but he gave his new friends anything they wanted – there were sugary yellow drinks and yellow cakes.

The sun's children all danced and invited Brian to join them. There was a choir of yellow canaries and they all whistled and cheeped in tune.

At last, Brian thought he'd better go home. When they got back to earth, it was night and the stars and moon were bright in the sky. Little grey mouse was sure she had dreamed it all – but on her fur was a little yellow spot, gold like the sun, to prove it hadn't been a dream.

79

The Red Balloon

Francis had a lovely red balloon.

One morning he went for a walk in the wood. The path led through a carpet of soft grasses and fragrant flowers of every colour.

He picked some for his Mother. The red balloon rolled along at his feet then went on ahead. A squirrel saw it and followed it. Then the magpie, the jay and the robin all played with it.

The balloon saw a puddle of water and decided to take a swim, but he got very muddy.

Francis chased after his balloon and seeing how dirty it had got he washed it. Then they all played with the balloon.

The sun began to set, the birds all flew away to their nests, and the squirrel jumped up into his oak tree for the night.

Francis ran back home with his red balloon. Along his way, lots of little green frogs croaked, 'Goodnight Francis, goodnight little red balloon. Come and play in the wood again tomorrow.'

And Francis promised that they would.

80

The Cat and the Seagull

'Miaou! Miaou!' cried the little lost cat. 'Help! I'm all alone in the wind on the beach!'

The little cat ran along the dunes, in and out of the waving grasses, looking for his master.

He forgot his misery for a moment while he played with the white wavelets.

But then the wind blew more strongly and he shivered in his wet fur.

At last, he found an old boat and crept underneath it and lay on the sand.

'Where are you?' cried the seagull. 'Where are you, little cat?'

Then the little cat saw the seagull hop under the boat and join him, and they huddled together to keep warm.

When the sun came out again, the seagull took the little cat back home.

The Secret of Nicola and Oliver

'Nicola? Nicola! Where are you?' called Oliver.

Nicola was down in the cellar and she said, 'I'm here – come and see what I've found!'

In a dark corner of the cellar, they found an old Christmas tree.

'There's a lorry coming soon to take it away,' said Oliver.

'Oh, what a shame – it did look so nice with its decorations!' said Nicola.

Then she said, 'No, I don't want my little Christmas tree taken away!'

'Look,' said Oliver, 'it's still got all its roots – let's hide it away!'

'What a good idea,' said Nicola.

'Let's put it in a box at the far end of the cellar,' Oliver said.

Nicola went upstairs and a few minutes later came back carrying a big box.

The children picked up the little Christmas tree and put it in the box.

'Now, we must find some earth and put it in the box,' said Oliver.

They went upstairs and emptied some earth from the flower pots.

'What are you doing?' asked their Mother.

'Oh, we're just clearing up a bit,' they replied.

But the little tree still didn't have enough earth for its roots.

So the children went into the forest and dug up lots of earth and dead leaves.

'Oh good,' said Nicola, 'the box is full now. I'll give my little tree some water every day!'

'Let's open the window in here,' said

Oliver, 'then the sun will warm it up, and the mice and spiders can come in and keep it company.'

Then, one day, Daddy said, 'I'm going to take this old cupboard down to our cellar.'

'Oh, Daddy, we'd better come with you,' cried Nicola and Oliver.

'Hallo,' said Daddy, 'I must have got the wrong cellar – we don't have any trees in store in our cellar!'

'Daddy, look Daddy, it's our little Christmas tree, our little tree which we want to keep alive!'

'Well, you are a funny lot,' said Daddy, 'you ought to have told me. Trees don't live in the dark like mushrooms – they need light and air!'

Nicola began to cry.

'Come on, silly, cheer up – I'll get a big trailer and we'll take the tree into the forest and plant it properly.'

And soon, in the green and sunny forest where the wind told stories about the spring, the little Christmas tree took root and spread its branches wide, and all the birds came to have a look at it.

When Christmas time came round again, Nicola and Oliver went to the forest to visit the little tree. Snow was falling gently on its branches.

'That's Nature's way of decorating it for Christmas,' said Nicola. 'How pretty it looks!'

And the little tree shook with happiness.

82

Rosalie and the Little Fish

Rosalie was a little cat with red and black striped fur. She was very fond of tiptoeing across the soft grass on the lawn, towards the little pond in the middle where the goldfish swam.

She used to hide under the biggest leaf she could find, just at the edge of the pond, and wait patiently till the goldfish came into view.

As soon as she saw it she would put her paw quickly into the water, all her claws ready and try to catch the fish. The little cat would lick her lips thinking of the meal that would follow.

But the goldfish wasn't so silly as that. He knew when the cat was there, and he swam off under the reeds to safety.

Rosalie, very disappointed, went away, hoping that next time she would be lucky.

But the little goldfish knew that Rosalie wouldn't catch him. There were lots of places to hide in the pond!

83

The Angry Old Fence

'I've had enough of you climbing all over me and damaging my planks,' said the old fence to some naughty schoolboys. 'You use me as a swing, you rattle me about and I shall fall to pieces if you don't stop it,' he finished in despair.

When the boys had gone, the fence took a good look at himself in the farmyard pond. 'Tomorrow, the farmer will come along with a hammer and nails and mend me again,' he moaned. 'I don't think I can take any more of this treatment.'

That evening, the old fence pulled up all his posts and putting his planks under his arm, walked off.

The old fence walked on until he came to the beach and said, 'My! Isn't the sea beautiful!'

The old fence put down his posts and built himself along the seashore.

One day, an old lady was walking along the beach.

'That's a beautiful old fence,' she said. 'You come with me and I'll put you in my garden.'

Now the old fence still gets climbed upon, but not by naughty boys. The old lady's roses climb gently round his wooden posts and make him feel so happy!

84

The Round Island

On a little round island there lived a little donkey, who was soon tired of going round and round the little round island.

He decided to leave the island.

The seagull advised him not to. 'We're happy here – why don't you stay?'

But the donkey didn't listen. He swam away through the blue sea.

He landed on a beach where some kindly rabbits gave him some carrots.

Then, the farmer arrived.

The rabbits all ran away and hid in their hutches.

The farmer put a rope round the little donkey's neck and decided that he'd make the donkey work.

He made him pull heavy weights and never gave him enough to eat.

There was a little boy on the farm also, and he, too, had to work hard.

He and the donkey became good friends.

One day, the nasty farmer fell ill, and all the animals ran away from the farm and went back to the little round island where they were all very happy.

85

The Little Crab

'Don't leave the hole, little crab,' said Mother Crab to her small son. 'There are children about with fishing nets.'

But the little crab climbed out of his hole.

'Oh, look!' cried the children. 'A crab!'

'Quick, catch him!' they shouted.

Mother Crab pulled her son down into the hole just in time. The children tried digging up the sand but they were too late – little crab was safe!

86

Coffee-with-Cream

'Look, everyone – isn't it marvellous! I've found a little dog that was lost! I shall call him Coffee-with-cream,' said Anne.

'That's a silly name,' said Roland, 'you might as well call it Onion-soup!'

'We'll all go to the Fair,' said Mummy.

The children enjoyed themselves at the Fair and they ate lots of sausages.

Anne suddenly dashed into the crowd.

'Coffee-with-cream, where are you?' she called.

A little boy was welcoming the dog with open arms and saying, 'Biscuit, look Daddy, I've found Biscuit!' And the little boy said, 'Biscuit, you naughty dog, I shall keep you on a lead in future.'

Anne burst into tears.

'Wait a moment,' said Daddy, 'we'll think of something.'

'Impossible,' said Anne. 'We can't each have half of the dog!'

The little boy came up and said, 'If you like, we'll both take it in turns with him.'

Anne felt better. She had found Coffee-with-cream and found a new friend as well.

87

Ragtime's Adventure

Ragtime was a rascal of a puppy. He knew every muddy puddle there was to paddle in and every cat there was to chase for miles around.

One day, a man arrived in the garden to paint the fence. He had brought two large brushes and a pot of sticky brown paint.

'Now keep out of mischief,' warned his little mistress, who could see Ragtime eyeing the brushes.

'Yes, keep out of mischief,' teased a pussy cat, perched on a low branch of a tree, overhanging the fence.

That was too much for Ragtime. He meant to teach that cheeky cat a lesson. He scrambled on to the fence, lost his balance and tumbled off again, right into the pot of sticky brown paint.

Rascally puppies are always in trouble – now Ragtime is in it up to his ears!

88

The Paint-Box Fairies

Do you like painting pictures? Jenny did. She used every scrap of paper she could find in the house to draw and paint on.

One day, her uncle came to visit and brought Jenny a box of paints. 'They are rather special,' he said mysteriously.

Jenny could not wait to use them. She found a sheet of paper in her room, filled a jar with water and got her brushes.

Now what could she paint? She opened the paint-box and, as she did so, it seemed to say, 'paint some butterflies.'

In no time at all, Jenny had painted two butterflies, so beautifully, that she could hardly believe her eyes.

Then, as she sat back to admire her work, the butterflies flew off the paper!

No sooner had that happened, when the paint-box seemed to be telling her to paint some birds.

Jenny quickly found some more paper and set to work again. First she painted a bluebird and then two more birds.

Never had Jenny painted birds so delicately before and, when they were finished, she sat back to admire her work. As she did so, the birds fluttered their wings and flew off the paper.

Jenny followed the birds and the butterflies outside and met her uncle, who was walking in the garden.

'I told you the paint-box was special,' he laughed. 'Those creatures are really the paint-box fairies in disguise. Every time you paint something with wings, you may be sure it will fly away.'

So, the next time you see a creature with tiny wings – look carefully – it may be one of Jenny's paintings!

89

Two Kittens

Mummy cat lovingly licked and cleaned her two little black kittens, Puff and Scuff.

'How am I going to tell them apart?' wondered Mummy cat. 'I've already washed *that* one – or was it *this* one?'

The two kittens rolled and tumbled about and got so mixed up that Mummy cat couldn't tell one from the other.

'Here, Puff,' called Mummy. They both went up to her.

'Scuff, come here,' said Mummy, and again both kittens went up to her.

'I know what we'll do,' said Mummy cat. 'I'll tie a piece of red ribbon to *this* one, and a piece of blue ribbon to *that* one, then I'll know which is Puff and which is Scuff!'

63

90

The Little Giraffe

Once, there was a little giraffe called George, who lived with his Mother and Father in a National Park in Africa.

One hot sunny afternoon, George and his Mother were nibbling at some juicy leaves, growing at the top of a tree.

Along the dusty road came a big truck carrying a very important film producer and his camera crew. They stopped to take some pictures of George and his Mother. Suddenly, a gusty breeze blew the film producer's hat off, which landed in the very tree George was eating!

George was about to take a mouthful of hat to see what it tasted like, when his Mother stopped him.

'Give it back to the gentleman, dear,' she said. 'Hats don't taste very nice.'

George did as he was told.

The producer was so pleased that he promised to make George the star of his new film, which was all about the Park.

'This is one day I won't forget in a hurry,' said George proudly.

'And I don't suppose the producer will either,' laughed his Mother. 'He nearly lost his hat!'

91

Big Sister

Mary was six and her big sister was sixteen.

Mary didn't like her sister being so much, much older than she was because they could never play at dolls or hop-scotch together.

Her big sister would always say, 'I'm too old for those games – and I haven't got the time anyway!'

Mothers' Day was coming soon. Mary had a present for her Mother but it was in a plain box, so she decided to paint a picture on it. Then, suddenly the paint-brush slipped and the picture was ruined!

Seeing her little sister's tears, big sister simply had to help her. She took the paintbrush and went to work on Mary's picture. Soon, it looked marvellous.

'What luck to have a big sister after all!' thought Mary.

92

April Fool!

It was April Fools' Day and Mark cut out a fish from a piece of cardboard and hung it on his sister's back.

Then, when she went out for a walk he walked along behind, laughing at the comments made by passers-by.

But he soon noticed that they weren't laughing at her, but at him.

Then someone called out, 'Hallo, donkey!' and when he looked behind him, he saw that somebody had pinned a cardboard donkey on to his own back!

'He who laughs last laughs longest!' said his sister. 'April Fool!'

Spring and the Mole

Mrs Mole didn't feel sleepy any more.

'It must be the spring poking through,' she said.

She looked round for her glasses, but she had mislaid them during her long winter sleep. She couldn't find them anywhere, so she decided to poke her nose out of doors just as she was.

The sun was shining, the sky was blue and the sparrows were cheeping and hopping about in Frances's garden.

'Cheep! Cheep!' said the sparrows. 'It's spring at last Mrs Mole!'

'I can't see a thing,' said Mrs Mole, who was very short-sighted and still hadn't found her glasses, 'but it doesn't matter – I'll go on ahead and meet the spring myself.'

And she trotted off down the path in Frances's garden.

'Miaou!' called the cat. 'Where are you going in such a hurry, Mrs Mole?'

Down in the forest, the squirrels and weasels and all the birds were playing games, but not the blackbird – she was busy building her nest.

The mole could smell the first scents of spring, but this wasn't enough – she wanted to see it.

If only she could have her glasses!

A kindly oriole lent her a pair, which had belonged to her Grandmother.

The mole trotted on to meet the spring – and there he was at last! Just a little boy, with lots of daisies in his arms.

'How happy I am to see you at last!' said Mrs Mole, and she danced a few steps with the little boy.

'Cuckoo!' called the cuckoo. 'Let's play hide-and-seek, shall we?'

The mole liked this idea and she went and hid in lots of places in the forest, but the cuckoo always found her.

At last, tired out with so much running, Mrs Mole went back to the garden where Frances was waiting for her.

Mrs Mole was given a little corner of the garden all to herself.

Hooray for the spring!

94

The Little Brown Lamb

One fine morning, the little brown lamb went for a walk.

'Where are you going, little brown lamb, where are you going?' everyone asked.

But he didn't answer and kept on walking until he came to the village school.

He knocked on the door.

'Come in, little brown lamb, what do you want?' asked the schoolmaster.

'I want to learn to read, please.'

'Then sit down on the bench and listen.'

That evening, the little brown lamb went back up the hill to rejoin his brothers and sisters.

'What have you been doing, little brown lamb?' they asked.

But he didn't answer. He just dreamed.

And then, one day, the little brown lamb brought back from school a big book full of stories and pictures.

'Come and sit down,' he said to them all. 'I'm going to read you a lovely story.'

And so it was that every evening all the little lambs sat round him before bedtime and listened while he read them a story from the big book.

95

A Beam of Moonlight

One scented spring night a beam of moonlight came down to Earth. He danced around the silent farmyard for a while, then he awoke a large, fat hen. 'Is it daylight already?' clucked the sleepy hen.

Next, the beam of moonlight visited the sow and her piglets. 'It's too early to be woken up,' she snorted.

The beam of moonlight was quite upset. He couldn't understand why no one was pleased to see him.

'Perhaps the cock will be happy to see me,' he said. 'He always rises early.'

'Cock-a-doodle-doo,' crowed the cock angrily. 'It's too early even for me!'

And, of course, he woke everyone up.

The mischievous beam of moonlight decided to go back and join the stars. He was beginning to feel sleepy anyway!

96

The Pansies and the Spring Ball

Snug in their little pots, the young pansies weren't happy at all. They wanted to go to the Spring Ball. But, how could they get there?

Little George took them all out and set them free in the wood.

The sparrow started looking for the squirrel's trumpet – he was always losing it! The blackbirds and finches began tuning up their instruments.

The frog practised a few high jumps – he was going to give a performance in public so he wanted to be at his best.

A young lily-of-the-valley and an iris told the young pansies that they looked very nice.

George gave them all a wash in the pond so that their roots were quite clean.

A toad put on a beautiful bow tie.

The nasturtiums led the pansies towards the clearing where the roses, the tulips, the periwinkles and the irises and lilies were all waiting.

Then the crickets struck up the first bars of the dance.

The pansies danced round with the irises, the cuckoo danced with the frog, and said, 'Let's get married.'

'Spendid idea!' said the owl, and the blackbird married them straight away.

All the flowers danced round the merry couple and wished them happiness.

The morning came and George went to collect the young pansies, who were very tired after dancing such a lot and drinking lots of apricot nectar.

As soon as George had planted them back in their little pots, they fell asleep.

What a marvellous evening – they would never forget it!

101

Round and Round

In a little round garden, there was a little round fishpond filled with clear water. And in the pond there lived three goldfish. The house at the top of the garden had a round tower.

There were two little boys there, both quite round.

They had a ball, with a red stripe on it just the colour of the goldfish.

The two little boys were as round as their ball, as the pond and as the garden itself.

One day, the boys floated their ball on the pond and the goldfish were very pleased because they could play with it now.

The little boys and the goldfish all played with the ball on the round pond.

When the evening came, everybody was very tired and they all went to bed.

The ball stayed on the pond all night.

Tomorrow, the little boys would play with the ball and the goldfish again.

102

Mr and Mrs Robin

'Spring is here, every bird must be married,' said the Sun.

So the robin put on his best feathers, the white and the red and the brown, and hopped away to whistle gaily to little Miss Robin up at her window.

Miss Robin loved the robin's song and joined in the chorus with him.

A few weeks later the Sun received an invitation to their wedding. He had been to lots of weddings that spring, but Mr and Mrs Robin's was the best!

71

The Little Bell

Once, a long time ago, in a country far away, there stood a magnificent cathedral. High in the belltower, the bells peeled out their joyful message and all who came to visit the cathedral, returned with its magical music ringing in their ears.

That was all a long time ago. The cathedral has long since been destroyed, by fire and wind and time itself. All that remains is the smallest bell that had once rung so proudly from its lofty tower.

The little bell lies on a village green, in the place where the cathedral once stood. One Easter, a curious thing happened, and this is the story . . .

One Easter Sunday, just as all the village children were going home from church, they heard a bell ringing, so beautifully, that they stopped to listen. It seemed that the sound was coming from the village green and, when they ran there, they found the little bell ringing all by itself!

Imagine how surprised they were. As the children approached the little bell, the ringing faded away, then, to their utter amazement, they found that it was filled to the brim with Easter chocolates – chocolate eggs and fish all neatly tied with ribbons – enough for every boy and girl and all the village folk, too!

It was an astonishing story for people to believe – some did and some didn't. But that is the story of the little bell and no one has been able to explain it to this day.

Christine and Sarah

Christine was eight years old, so her Mummy decided to give her a party. Two boys who could play guitars came along as well and all the children danced to their merry tunes.

Suddenly, Christine saw two big tears roll down the cheeks of her friend Sarah.

Her Mummy was ill in bed and Sarah was worried about her.

So Christine filled a bag with gifts, and cakes and little sweets and said to Sarah, 'Run quickly back home and give these to your Mummy – we mustn't forget her while we're all having fun here this afternoon!'

And Sarah was sure that such a nice gesture would make her Mummy feel better at once.

And it did!

★ **105**

The Squirrel

Very soon, if you're quick,
You'll see Mister Redtail flickity-flick,
Skip and scuttle, snap and scurry;
Why is he always in a hurry?
Flippity-flash and flounce and fuss,
Why won't he stop and talk to us?

 **106**

A Surprise for the Farmer's Wife

 **107**

Mimi the Turtledove

Mrs Larkin, the farmer's wife, bought a new hen. She called it Eggity Peggity.

On the first day, Mrs Larkin went to the henrun. There were lots of eggs there but none from Eggity Peggity.

On the second day, Mrs Larkin collected fresh eggs from all her hens, except from Eggity Peggity. But on the third day, when Mrs Larkin went to collect the eggs, she caught Eggity Peggity escaping through a hole in the henrun.

'Well,' said Mrs Larkin. 'No wonder I can't find any eggs from Eggity Peggity. She is laying them all outside!' So Mrs Larkin set off with her basket and she found one egg by the pigsty, one by the milk churns and two more in the field.

Eggity Peggity still lays her eggs around the farm. 'She lays them in such funny places,' says Mrs Larkin, 'that she never fails to surprise me!'

Mimi felt very lonely by herself in the house.

She hopped up on to the sill of the open window and then flew round in the sun. She went to the park and there she met a grey pigeon. They chatted together and strolled about among the flowering trees.

Soon it was time for Mimi to return home. She told the grey pigeon where she lived and the grey pigeon promised to visit her every week.

Now Mimi wouldn't be lonely anymore.

109

Nolly the Elf and Roger

One fine day, Nolly the elf decided to play a trick on Roger.

He cast a spell on him and made him clasp his arms behind his back.

Roger had to carry his school satchel home on his head.

His Mother called the doctor, who said he'd never treated such a complaint, and he would call back the next day to see if Roger was any better.

During the night the wise old owl scolded Nolly and said that he must remove the spell.

When the doctor called, he was surprised to hear from Roger's Mother that Roger had already left for school, swinging his satchel above his head with both hands!

108

A Beautiful Baby

Daddy and Mummy were very happy. 'We'll be having a little baby in the spring!' they told all their friends.

The grannies and the aunties all got to work knitting baby clothes and soon they filled all the drawers in the nursery.

In the spring the flowers blossomed, the birds sang and baby Helen came into the world. How happy Mummy and Daddy were with their new baby.

Everybody came to admire Helen in her little red cot which was trimmed with ribbons.

'Doesn't she look like her Father?' some said.

'Doesn't she look like her Mother?' said others.

'What a funny little nose,' they said.

'What a nice little face,' said the neighbours.

But the most delighted person of all was Helen's brother John, who stood looking on very quietly while all the neighbours chatted together. He didn't have anything to say. He just felt very pleased to have a baby sister and a new playmate.

110

The Goat on the Roof

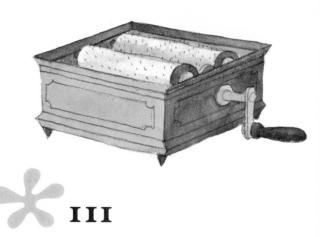

'I'm off to the market,' said Mrs Goat to her daughter Cecily. 'Be good while I'm gone.'

'I will, Mummy,' said Cecily.

There was an old house by the road whose roof was covered with grass. Cecily trotted up to it and saw that there was a ladder against the wall.

She climbed the ladder and was soon on the roof – what delicious grass!

Roland the fox was out walking and saw her on the roof.

'I'll play a trick on her,' thought Roland, so he took the ladder away from the house, and then ran away laughing!

Cecily found that she couldn't get down and the little goat called for help.

Fortunately, the old shepherd wasn't far away and heard her cries. He replaced the ladder and climbed up on to the roof.

He picked the little goat up in his arms and carried her down to the ground safely.

Cecily would not climb on to any roofs again!

111

The Music Box

Steve and Emma decided to clean out their cupboard, from top to bottom.

'What a nice surprise for Mummy when she gets back,' said Emma.

Then, down amongst all the woollen vests and winter clothes what a surprise they had – they found an old music box that had once belonged to Grannie.

She had looked for it for days, but never found it.

So they decided that evening they would hide the little music box underneath one of the napkins on the dinner table, so that when Grannie picked up her napkin, she would find it there.

Emma said to Steve, 'You see, Steve, it is a good thing to have a clear out now and again. You never know what you will find!'

Pip the Squirrel

Pip the little squirrel had been hidden away during the winter in his hole in the old oak tree at the bottom of Grandfather's garden.

He had slept all winter, waking for a few hours at a time to eat acorns from his store, all neatly stacked away in his pantry.

But winter was very long and Pip was a hungry little squirrel.

One fine morning, he saw that he had very little left for the rest of the winter. He would have to find food somewhere.

What should he do?

It was then that he saw Grandfather in his garden, carrying baskets of apples up from the cellar.

He watched him coming and going, now with a basket of pears now another of apples.

What a temptation for the hungry little squirrel! But he knew it was not nice to steal so he just settled down to wait until something turned up.

Fortunately, it did. Grandfather had seen the little squirrel lots of times and he knew that his store of nuts must be getting very low. So he left a few apples and other tasty morsels at the bottom of the old oak tree for Pip to come down and take.

In the spring, Pip repaid Grandfather's kindness by coming and sitting next to him on the garden bench and amusing him with his pranks.

One good turn deserves another!

Lotus Flower and Her Friends

The cherry trees were all in blossom in Lotus Flower's garden.

On her birthday, the little girl invited her friends along.

The little Japanese girls all came and greeted each other and then sat round the lacquered table for tea, with lots of delicious cakes.

Then they all played hide-and-seek in the garden, and laughed as they took turns on the swing.

They sang and danced.

When the sun went down, the little guests went home.

Lotus Flower admired the doll they had brought her.

She washed up the cups and plates – there were a lot of them!

She was very happy. She had had a wonderful birthday!

114

Barbara's Straw Hat

It was a warm sunny day, so Barbara decided to eat her picnic lunch in the green field behind the farm.

She took off her beautiful straw hat and placed it carefully on the grass. It was a birthday present from Grandma and she was so pleased with it.

She started her lunch and Biscuit the goat, who was standing nearby, looked on enviously.

She was so hungry. And goats love straw!

Suddenly, Biscuit rushed up to the hat, took it in her mouth, and bounded away.

'Biscuit! Biscuit!' cried Barbara. 'Give it back to me at once!'

The goat munched and munched. The green ribbons and the red flowers were particularly delicious!

115

Two Friends in a Boat

Bill, the little dog, had been invited by his friend, Kiki the seal, to go sailing.

Kiki was a good sailor. But Bill wasn't and it took him three tries before he even managed to get into the boat.

Using an oar, Kiki rowed away from the shore. The wind grew stronger and the little boat began to sail, while Kiki pulled on different ropes.

Bill wondered how his friend knew which was which. There were ropes everywhere!

Then Kiki handed over the tiller to his friend to steer the boat.

The boat went faster and faster and sailed further away from the shore, then, all of a sudden, Bill pulled on the wrong rope and a huge wave made the boat turn over.

Bill didn't know how to swim, so Kiki put him on his back and they got to the shore safely.

A friendly sailor towed the sailing boat back to the shore.

'I think,' said Bill to Kiki, 'I will learn to swim before I go sailing again.'

116

Lesson From a Parrot

Joseph didn't know how to talk properly – he just used to shout!

He shouted all the time, sometimes for no reason at all, and no one could get him to stop.

Then his Uncle Matthew had an idea: he would buy Joseph a parrot and teach him phrases like, 'Joseph shouts all the time!' Or, 'Joseph, you do make a noise with your shouting!'

Then Uncle Matthew gave the parrot to young Joseph. When he called again, a couple of months later, Joseph's Mother said to him, 'Joseph doesn't shout any more now. He has become very good indeed. In fact he speaks so softly and politely that the parrot has learnt to say, "Joseph, can you speak a little louder, please. I can't hear you!"'

Crystal-Gazing

Sounds the Same

Binny picked up a coloured ball, wound a red turban round her head and said, 'I'm crystal-gazing, look at me!'

'What can you see?' asked Mops the cat.

'I can see a large, red rose which has just opened its petals,' said Binny.

'Then it must be spring,' said Mops. 'What else?'

'And now I can see blue butterflies and some pink ones too, flying across the fields and round the lambs,' replied Binny.

'It's definitely spring,' said Mops.

'Now I can see a bowl of milk for you, Mops, and a lovely rich cake that Mummy has just made for me!'

The crystal-gazer put down her crystal ball, and ate a piece of cake while Mops drank her milk.

Then the little girl and her cat went out into the garden to see the beautiful red rose, and then into the field where they watched lovely butterflies which were all around them.

Binny laughed and danced for joy. She danced with Mops, and then with a tiny lamb who'd been born the day before!

A plumber could mend one – but you could eat this!

Two alike make one of these – but this one is a fruit.

Some kings and queens do this for years but this would make them wet!

Solution: leak, leek, pair pear, rain reign.

The White Goat

'Little white goat,' said the shepherd, 'I'm going to trust you to look after my flock of sheep this evening – I'm off to the village dance.'

'All right,' said the goat, 'you have a good time – I'll watch over the sheep.'

Little white goat was so busy watching the flock that she didn't notice her little black kid stray away over the mountain.

Little black kid had never been out at night on his own. He felt very adventurous.

He made his way down to the river's edge, nibbled at the grass, and drank from the cool water.

Suddenly a shadow loomed up behind him. It was a large wolf. Little black kid didn't know what to do. He was very frightened. But his Mother, who had been searching for him, saved him.

She lowered her horns and charged. The wolf tried to bite her with his big teeth, but the little white goat butted him into the river!

The little white goat went back to guarding the flock and little black kid decided to stay closer to his Mother in future.

120

The Swing

'Swing me very high up,' said Helen to Oliver. 'Push the swing much higher!'

The swing went so high it touched the top of the hedge.

'Higher, higher still!' called Helen.

Oliver gave a mighty push and then there was a snapping sound – the rope had broken!

Helen landed head first in a field of hay.

'I think I'll use that broken rope for skipping,' said Helen to Oliver. 'It's safer on the ground!'

121

Luke's Many-coloured Ball

Luke was given a beautiful coloured ball for his birthday. The boy and his coloured ball became inseparable.

But, one morning, Luke gave his ball so hard a kick that it went right across a field, down a bank and into a car that was speeding along the road.

When Luke arrived, all out of breath, at the top of the bank, he was just in time to see the car going out of sight!

Luke *was* upset. So his Mother gave him another present, but nothing could console him for the loss of his favourite ball.

Then, one day, a car stopped at Luke's house and an old gentleman got out to ask the way to town.

Luke gave him full directions and the old gentleman was so pleased that he said, 'Thank you, my boy, and as a reward, here's a coloured ball that fell out of the sky into my car the other day!'

'Oh! My ball has come back!' cried Luke happily. 'I thought I had lost forever my favourite birthday present. Thank you. Next time I won't kick it quite so hard.'

Shy

Think of the timid violet
If you are very shy.
When strangers speak,
She drops her head
And whispers in reply.
But, when they've gone,
I'm sure she plays
And sings a playtime
song ;
I'm sure she's noisy
with her friends
And chatters all day
long !

123

Tiny the Naughty Squirrel

Mother Squirrel tucked her little son into his bed and said, 'Now, you stay in your warm bed and tomorrow that nasty cold will have gone.'

Tiny wriggled down further under the bedclothes and went off to sleep.

Mother Squirrel went out to do her shopping.

Tiny woke up and looked out of the window.

'My! Look at that lovely sun – I'm going out!' he said.

He jumped out of bed and dashed outside to play with his friends. What fun they all had!

'Goodness! Tiny, you do look pale – and you're shivering! What's the matter with you?' said his friends.

Tiny's teeth were chattering with cold.

'Quickly, Tiny, go back to your bed.'

When Mother Squirrel got back home, she found Tiny fast asleep, warm as toast under his favourite coloured quilt.

124

Susan and Tulip the Kitten

One fine day, Susan was playing in a field full of flowers.

'Ooh, look!' she cried, 'there's a little black ball in among the tulips!'

She tiptoed up to the little black ball and when she bent down to have a closer look, she saw that it was a fluffy little kitten.

She stroked him and he woke up, yawned, and blinked his green eyes.

'I shall call you Tulip,' said Susan.

She picked him up and took him into the house to show her Mummy.

'Now, Susan,' said her Mummy, 'I don't want that kitten to go jumping onto tables or tearing my curtains!'

'I promise you I'll watch him,' said Susan.

But the first thing Tulip did was to get all tied up in Mummy's knitting. Then he jumped on all the beds in turn, and settled down on the most comfortable one!

And then he went jumping about on the chairs and table and he knocked a plate off the table. Crash!

'No, darling,' said Mummy, 'you must take your little kitten outside. He's making a mess in the house!'

Susan was rather upset, but she took Tulip outside and let him run about on the sunny lawn. How happy he was now! He dashed about chasing butterflies and played hide-and-seek with shafts of sunlight.

'He's happier here,' said Susan.

And Susan's Mummy was happier too!

125
A Lollipop for Jolly

Jolly, the little bear, could not go to the fair. He had hurt one of his paws. But Bella, his little sister, had been with Mummy and told him all about it.

'I wish I had been there,' said Jolly.

'But I've brought something back for you,' said Bella. 'A large striped lollipop!'

Now Jolly didn't mind that he hadn't been to the fair!

 **126**

A Juicy Bone

'I don't want to be washed, and bathed and combed and all dressed up for the Dog Show,' said Scruffy, the little black and white dog. 'I want to be a real dog.'

'Come now, Scruffy,' said his mistress, 'you must not fuss so much – why, you'll be the most beautiful dog at the Show and will win first prize!'

'I don't care,' said Scruffy. 'I want to be free and happy.'

And since his mistress didn't understand him, Scruffy ran away as quickly as he could into the garden.

'Naughty Scruffy!' cried his mistress. 'You'll only have water for supper!'

Scruffy didn't mind at all. He went into his favourite corner of the garden and dug up a large juicy bone that he had been saving. It was delicious!

127

The Swallows Come Back in the Spring

One evening, when she got back from school, Christine saw a small blue bundle lying on the ground in front of her house. As she got closer she found that it was a swallow which had been hurt.

The little girl picked it up and took it inside to put it into a soft nest which she made.

She looked after it carefully and soon the bird was well again. But day by day the swallow lost its appetite and became very sad. Christine's Mummy put the cage in front of the open window.

She thought the fresh air would do the swallow good.

But when Christine got back from school that day, the swallow had flown away.

One morning, very early, Christine was woken up by a tap, tap, tap on her window. It was the swallow! And every morning after that, he came back to see his friend Christine.

When the summer was nearly over, all the swallows got ready to migrate to hotter countries for the winter.

Christine's swallow came and perched on her shoulder to say goodbye, and she was absolutely certain that she would see her little swallow next year.

128

Isabel's Hat

Isabel was showing off her new straw hat.

'Come and play with us, Isabel!' called her friends.

Isabel laid her new hat carefully down on the grass and went off to play.

'Where's my hat gone?' she asked when they had finished.

Nobody could find it anywhere, but the little grey donkey had a gleam in his eye – he had eaten it!

'It was very tasty,' he said. 'Thank you!'

Ricky the Shrewmouse

'I'm going to move house,' said Ricky the little shrewmouse to her friend the marmot, 'the food's all the same here!'

And in a flash, she had gone.

'Why run away when you can sleep?' cried the marmot, who sleeps all the time!

Crossing the wood, Ricky met a rabbit chewing some thyme.

'How can rabbits eat that? It stings like pepper!' said Ricky to herself.

'Are you eating flies?' she asked the frog by the pond.

'Yes, they're delicious – have some,' said the frog.

'I don't like them at all,' sighed Ricky, and went on her way.

'What are you nibbling?' she asked the squirrel.

'Hazelnuts, of course,' answered the squirrel. 'Try some.'

'Thank you. My! What funny things other people eat,' said the shrewmouse, 'and now I've broken a tooth!'

'Ah, you've come back then,' yawned the marmot, 'and with one tooth less and a tummy ache!'

'I think,' said the shrewmouse, 'that I prefer the food we find here. But, you know, one has to try everything once!'

130

Charlie the Lazy Snail

Daddy and Mummy snail slept with their three little ones close by. The sun was shining and it wasn't the right moment to go for a walk. But then it started to rain.

'The rain at last!' cried Charlie's two brothers. 'Let's all go for a walk.'

What fun they had, sliding over wet stones, drinking raindrops on the leaves and tumbling about in the little pools left by the rain!

'Where's Charlie?' asked Mummy snail suddenly. 'We must have lost him on the way here – we must find him.'

'Have you seen Charlie?' Daddy snail asked the lizard. But the lizard hadn't seen him. Neither had the frog nor the grass snake.

What do you think the snails found when they got back to their own little patch of garden?

Lazy Charlie was still asleep where they had left him. He poked out first one horn, then another, then opened one eye.

'I think it is raining,' he said. 'What about going for a walk?' he asked.

131

Market Day

To market, to market,
For good things to eat;
Crisp juicy apples,
Pears ripe and sweet.
A bag of best oatmeal,
A fresh currant bun.
Now home again, home again,
Shopping is done!

132

Hide-and-Seek

Six young rabbits were playing hide-and-seek.

'One, two, three! Your turn to seek!' said one of them to Bruno, the youngest.

His five little brothers all rushed away to hide in their favourite spot, where no one would find them, not even Bruno.

For hours, he searched far and wide, trying to find them. It was just as well that his Mother knew where everyone was hiding!

The evening came quickly and the five little rabbits, who were still waiting for Bruno to come and find them, began to get cold.

They all looked out from their hiding places and saw that little Bruno had vanished.

'But where could he be?' they asked their Mother.

'I know where he is,' she answered. 'He's down in our hole, nice and warm, and eating lettuce leaves – that will be a lesson to you all not to tease your little brother!'

133

Lily-of-the-Valley

Deep in a wood, hidden under the shade of a bush, Mary Caroline found the first tiny lily-of-the-valley of the year.

It was very pale and shaky with its little white bells scarcely open.

'Don't pick me,' it said to Mary Caroline, 'I'm so young.'

And Mary listened to what it said and left it there under the bush.

So the little flower lived a happy life with its roots down in nice, damp soil, while the breeze stirred the little white bells of its flowers.

Then, on the morning of one especially hot day, the little flower's time had come and it drooped and faded away.

134
Michael on the Moon

'One more rhyme before you go to sleep,' said Michael's Mother, tucking him into bed.

Michael turned the pages of his favourite nursery rhyme book. 'This one, please,' he said, and read it out loud:

I see the moon
And the moon sees me;
God bless the moon
And God bless me.

Then Michael went to sleep.

Or had he? For it seemed that he was out upon the rooftop, dressed in a space suit and helmet, ready for a trip to the moon! The moon came nearer and nearer until, bump, it landed on the chimney pots. The moon had a face with two twinkling eyes that sparkled with stars, and a mouth that was smiling and calling his name.

Michael awoke with a start. There were two twinkling eyes looking at him and there was a mouth, smiling and calling his name – but it wasn't the moon. It was Mummy, bending over his bed!

'Michael, Michael,' she called, softly. 'It's morning, and time to get up!'

135
Come Away With Me

Come child with me and find again in the breeze and the grasses, the ferns and the leaves, the land of childhood where we dream sweet dreams and all is magic.

Come child with me and we'll run together and chase the clouds to the edge of the sky and listen in the breeze to childhood dreams, and you'll be enchanted once more as you were before.

✳ 136

Golden Flame

One fine morning, in the middle of a great wood, with patches of yellow gorse, a little fox was born.

His Mother licked him, and nuzzled him, and called him Golden Flame.

One day, the little fox said, 'I want to go out alone now and see the wood and smell the honey and sniff the wild wind.'

Off he went, through the great wood.

'Goodness! That's a funny looking animal,' he said to himself.

It was a small, chubby boy.

Golden Flame snuggled up to him.

The boy stroked the little fox's ears and said, 'Stay with me and be my friend.' But just then, the owl hooted from the tree top, 'Run! Run! The hunters are coming!'

'Quick!' cried Anthony, 'let's run away!'

They reached the river's edge.

'We'll cross here – then the hunters and their dogs will lose your scent!'

Anthony waded across the river, holding the little fox securely in his arms until they reached the other side.

Then Anthony took Golden Flame home. The little fox had had enough adventures for one day!

 **137**

The Mischievous Star

Among the stars, the most mischievous was one called Stella.

One night, tired of the unending pranks played by this little star, the Queen of the Stars summoned Stella to her palace in the Milky Way and said, 'We are tired of your tricks. Only yesterday, I am informed, a traveller lost his way because you were not in your usual place in the heavens.'

And the Queen went on, 'You are banished from my realm. From now on, you will live on Earth. There the royal stables are awaiting the birth of a foal and you will adorn his brow.'

And when the foal was born he was ebony-black with a beautiful white star in the centre of his forehead.

The mischievous star was very happy. Now she wouldn't have to worry about being in the right place at the right time, because she would always be in the same place!

138
Prickly, the Little Hedgehog

Mrs Hedgehog was taking her four little hedgehogs for a walk through the woods.

'Today,' she said, as they shuffled along through the leaves, 'I am going to teach you how to roll into a ball. You must always do that if you feel danger is near,' she warned, 'then you will make it difficult for anything to harm you.'

Prickly, her youngest hedgehog thought that rolling into a tight, spiky ball was fun, and kept on doing it over and over again. Poor Mrs Hedgehog had to keep waiting for him to catch up.

On the way home, Prickly noticed two bright eyes looking at him from behind a bush. It was a big, hungry fox!

Quick as a flash, Prickly curled up in a tight little ball, just as his Mother had taught him.

'Ouch!' How that poor fox yelped as his long, soft nose buried itself in Prickly's sharp little spines.

'Well done!' said Prickly's Mother, when the fox had gone. 'What a good job you practised that lesson so well today!'

139
The Meringue Cake

Polly was playing with her toys, but she couldn't stop thinking about the meringue cake that her Mummy had made.

'I must try it,' she said, and went into the kitchen.

Just as she was picking up a spoon . . . the doorbell rang.

It was Daddy.

'What a delicious cake,' he said. 'I'm surprised Polly hasn't eaten it all.'

'Oh, no,' said Polly. 'Mummy and I were waiting for you. It's for our supper!'

Mick Makes Himself Useful

Mick was rather bored. It was a beautiful day, but nothing interested him at all. He was all on his own. His two friends, the cat and the little white lamb, had gone with the farmer in his old, creaking cart to visit the market.

'You must guard the farm,' said the farmer, 'while we're away. And don't do anything silly!'

Mick sulked and soon grew sleepy.

He slept for an hour or two, then awoke suddenly. And it was just as well that he did! There were two robbers inside the farm!

Mick bared his teeth, and rushed at them, barking loudly.

The two robbers scrambled over the wall, dropping their bags as they did so!

Mick had frightened them so much that they hadn't managed to steal a thing!

The farmer was pleased when he got back.

'For that, you shall come with me to visit the market next week,' said the farmer, as a special treat.

Hoppy the Kangaroo

Hoppy the little kangaroo was out for a a walk with his Mother.

'Mummy, I'm cold,' he said suddenly.

'Then you must jump into my pouch at once,' said his Mother.

Hoppy hopped inside and curled up inside his Mother's pouch.

'Where is Hoppy?' asked everyone when they got back home.

'He felt cold. He's gone inside my pouch to get warm again,' answered his Mother.

'Cold!' exclaimed everyone. 'On a fine, sunny day like this?'

Hoppy's Mother hadn't thought of that and she said, 'Yes, I think we'll call at the doctor's tomorrow.'

The next day, Hoppy was taken to see the doctor.

'Open your mouth, say 99, let's have a look at your tongue,' said the doctor. 'Now breathe in, out, in, out.' And the doctor examined Hoppy all over.

'Your son is in perfect health – all he needs is a lot more exercise in the fresh air. You must take him for long walks in the country and one day he'll be a fine, big, strong kangaroo!'

And ever since that day, Hoppy has never felt cold!

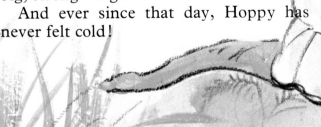

142

The Eagle and the Sparrow

'I'll bet you that despite the span of your great wings, I can fly higher than you,' said the sparrow to the eagle.

'I'll take your bet,' replied the eagle. 'But I'd like to see a bird as small as you fly as high in the sky as an eagle!'

'There's nothing to it,' said the sparrow. 'I'll show you.'

The eagle spread his great wings and took off. He flew higher and higher up into the blue sky, thinking that he'd left the little sparrow far below.

'I am the king of birds, and can fly higher than any other bird,' he cried.

'Cheep! Cheep! Here I am,' said the sparrow above him.

The eagle looked down and then to left and right, but he couldn't see the sparrow.

'Where are you?' he called.

'Here, above you, eagle,' said the sparrow.

The eagle was astonished. He couldn't fly any higher, so the sparrow had won.

And the secret was that the sparrow had hidden himself on the eagle's back. When the eagle had flown as high as he could, the sparrow had left the eagle's back and then flown still higher!

* 143

Please!

Mummy is busy,
Daddy's away,
Won't one of you
Come out and play
Hide-and-seek
With us today?

* 144

The Little Bird

It was Simon's birthday, but he was feeling miserable. He had a bad cold and his Mother had told him to stay in bed.

A little bird settled on his bedroom window-sill and began to sing. His song sounded just like, 'cheer up, cheer up, cheer up,' sung over and over again.

'Yes, I will cheer up,' laughed Simon. 'Your song has made me feel better already. In fact, I feel well enough to get up!'

An Adventurous Kitten

Misty was a beautiful light grey kitten with green eyes, and Angela had put a lovely blue ribbon round her neck.

Misty got bored on her own so she went into the wood next door to the farmhouse.

The paths were bordered with red and blue and yellow flowers, so Misty made up a posy for Angela, but she soon put her posy down when she heard some nestlings high up in an old oak.

Misty clawed her way up the tree towards the little birds and was just getting close to the nest when the Mother bird came back and squawked at the kitten, flapping her wings to frighten her away.

And she did – Misty backed away, slipped, missed her footing and fell a long, long way down. Fortunately, she landed on a bed of moss. She got a big bump on her head and felt dazed.

The frog gave her some first-aid and waved air at her with a waterlily leaf.

When night-time came, Misty went back home, where she was given some warm milk and fell asleep on Angela's lap.

Catherine and the Wolf

Catherine was going to a fancy dress party and she had decided to go as Little Red Riding Hood. When Mummy saw her she said, 'All you need now is a wolf, then you are sure to win first prize!'

Catherine set off through a little wood. Suddenly a young wolf appeared.

'Hello, Little Red Riding Hood,' said the wolf. 'I've heard a lot about you and your tasty, I mean, dear old Grandmother.'

'I'm not Little Red Riding Hood,' said Catherine, truthfully. 'I'm Catherine.'

'Oh,' said the wolf, disappointed.

'Are you the Big Bad Wolf?' asked Catherine, nervously.

'No,' answered the young wolf, honestly.

'Well then,' said Catherine, 'since I am only pretending to be Little Red Riding Hood, why don't you pretend to be the Big Bad Wolf and come to the party with me?'

The wolf thought that this was an excellent idea, so the two friends went to the party and won first prize!

147

So They Say

There is one magic day,
So they say . . . so they say . . .
When grasshoppers play
And pipe to the flowers
For hours and hours,
So they say . . . so they say . . .

 **148**

A Pretty Posy

Jenny and her sister, Kate, were staying with their three cousins who lived on a farm. One hot, sunny afternoon, the children went to play in the big meadow.

'Let's see how many different kinds of wild flowers we can find,' said Kate.

So the girls looked very carefully and picked just a few flowers each, so that there would be plenty left to grow. They found all sorts of lovely flowers – bright red poppies, golden dandelions and buttercups and some tiny blue forget-me-nots. Then the girls put them all together to make a pretty posy.

Sally, the youngest cousin said, 'Let's give the posy to Mummy. It will be a nice surprise for her.'

When they got home, Sally's Mummy put her pretty posy on the table. 'One nice surprise deserves another,' she said. 'I have a nice surprise for you, too. A fresh cream tea!'

The Little Robin

Jane and Simon found a little robin in the garden one day. The cat from next door had chased it and bruised its wing.

They took the little bird and, very gently, put it in an old bird cage in the garage. Soon the little robin was chirping to be let out! So Simon opened the cage door and the robin flew away.

'Will he come again?' asked Jane.

'I'm sure he will,' said Simon. 'And, when he does, we will make quite sure that the cat stays in his own garden!'

The Little Black Hen

Little black hen had never felt so happy. She had just laid her very first egg. There it lay among the golden straw, beautiful and perfectly shaped.

'Cluck! Cluck! Cluck!' she cried. 'I've laid an egg – it's for Graham.'

Graham was the little boy who came every day to collect the eggs from the chicken coop, and he saw that the little black hen had laid her first egg.

'Congratulations!' cried Graham. 'It's a beautiful egg – I shall have it tomorrow!'

'Cluck! Cluck! Cluck!' cried the little black hen, very proud and happy.

But the other chickens were all very upset – they also laid eggs for Graham, so why wasn't he congratulating them?

The little boy saw how they felt and he said to them, 'You mustn't be jealous. Your eggs are all very, very good. I'm congratulating the little black hen on her egg because it's the very first egg she's laid. But you are all wonderful chickens and I love you all just the same!'

The chickens understood at once, and tomorrow they would each lay a very large egg for Graham!

151

The Island With a Volcano

152

The Weathercock

On an island in the Pacific, John and Sandra lived happily among lots of brightly-coloured birds.

Their house was made of logs with palm fronds for a roof.

They lived on fruit, fish and shellfish.

One day, the volcano started to rumble and send up clouds of smoke.

John ran to it and said, 'You mustn't burn up our island!'

The volcano laughed – and instead of smoke he sent up lots of warm springs where everyone could bathe at just the right temperature.

The birds and the two children then went to see the volcano every day and so they got to know him better.

Summer came and stayed forever.

What a wonderful island!

There was once a fine church which had a tall steeple and, on top of that steeple, sat a very proud weathercock.

One day, two workmen came to look at the steeple. 'It's not safe,' said one. 'It will have to come down,' said the other. So the workmen took the steeple down and, with it, of course, the weathercock.

'That's not much use now,' said one workman. 'Throw it away.'

'I think I'll take it home for my little boy,' said the other. And he did.

The next day, the kind workman put a tall post in his garden, near some pretty hollyhocks. Then he fixed the weathercock on to the post and it spun round in the breeze, as good as before.

The workman's little boy was thrilled.

The weathercock was pleased, too.

'I may have come down in the world a bit,' he thought, 'but I'm much, much happier here.'

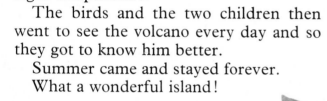

153

White Mouse Has Some Adventures

It was a beautiful morning and the little white mouse had had enough of being locked in her cage.

She managed to get the cage door open and scurried out to see the world. First, she crossed the tiles of the kitchen floor, then out into the garden.

The air was soft and warm and full of scents.

The little white mouse greeted several birds sitting on the garden wall, then she ran among the flowers and across the lawn.

Suddenly, she saw the big black cat approaching!

The little white mouse fled under a large lettuce leaf and hid there.

Verity, the old tortoise, stuck her head out and said, 'What are you doing in my lettuce patch?'

The little white mouse ran off to hide somewhere else.

Then, she walked all over Frank's feet while he was watering the garden.

'Naughty little white mouse,' he said. 'You ought to get back to your cage before you run into danger!'

Just then, the big black cat came back, licking his lips.

It was too much. Little white mouse climbed gratefully up into Frank's outstretched hand and was even more glad to be safely inside her cage.

'There's no place like home,' she sighed, as she nibbled a tasty piece of cheese.

154

The Little Fawn

'Go to sleep, little fawn,' said the doe.

But the little fawn had long wanted to see the woods by night and he waited until everyone was asleep. Then, he tiptoed outside without making a sound, trotted over the soft green moss and jumped with delight when he saw the stars, saying, 'Do stay there, dear stars, you're so beautiful!'

But the stars had to go and one by one they left the sky as the sun came up.

The little fawn went home, very tired, but very happy.

The Lazy Boy

There was once a boy called John Asleep. People called him that because he was so lazy. He wouldn't get up in the morning and he never helped his Mother at home.

One day, his Father said to him, 'I have had enough of your lazy ways. Now, my lad, help your Mother all you can or else I shall turn you out of this house!'

Soon afterwards, John Asleep's Mother asked him to go to the market and buy her a sack of corn. John Asleep's Father was nearby, so he went off willingly enough but, as he walked through the forest, the lazy boy sat down to rest. In a little while, an old man came along.

John Asleep had an idea. Clutching his ankle as though he were in great pain, he begged the old man to go to market for him and buy the sack of corn. The old man, believing the boy had injured his foot, took pity on him and agreed to help.

When the old man had gone, John Asleep lit a small fire and settled by it to sleep. As he slept, however, the fire caught at dried branches and leaves around it and, in no time at all, there was a blazing fire raging through the forest.

John Asleep awoke with a start and was terrified when he saw what he had done. Then he ran, as he had never run before, to get help. His Mother and his Father and all the townsfolk came with beaters and put out the flames.

Just as they were going home, they saw an old man struggling with a sack of corn on his back. How ashamed John Asleep was when he had to confess to his Mother and Father and all the townsfolk the trick he had played on the poor old man. And from that day to this, John Asleep has never been lazy again!

 **156**

The Little Caterpillar

The little caterpillar was most unhappy. He had eaten through a large leaf and now his skin was much too tight.

A fly flew past. 'Step out of that skin,' he said. 'You'll find you've got another one to wear, underneath!'

To his great surprise, the little caterpillar burst out of several skins. When he was fully grown, he shed his skin for the last time.

A beetle crawled by to see how he was getting on. He couldn't find the little caterpillar anywhere. Instead, he found a brown skin case, hanging from the stem of a plant by a silken thread.

An earthworm came along and explained. 'That's him, dangling from the plant, only now he's changed into a *pupa*. I'll tell you something else,' he went on secretly. 'At this very moment, he's turning into a butterfly!'

157

Hickety Pickety

Hickety, pickety, my fine hen,
She lays eggs for gentlemen;
Gentlemen come every day
To see what my fine hen doth lay.
Sometimes nine and sometimes ten,
Hickety, pickety, my fine hen.

158

Watching

*If you lie low and peep
    through grass
You can safely watch your
    enemies pass.
Keep quite still – don't
    twitch an ear –
Just in case the fox is
    near.
There's a rustling – who
    can it be?
It's only you just watch-
    ing me!*

159

Christian's Sandcastle

Christian was building a sandcastle on the beach.

When it was finished, he decorated it with lots of shells, of all sorts of colours and shapes.

During the night, a family of crabs decided to make the castle still stronger by adding lots of oyster shells to the top of the towers.

The next morning, Christian was surprised to see what his little friends had done for his castle.

Christian was very happy with it now and he played on the beach all day.

My Friend Sebastian

The Little Lamb

'Look!' cried the children, 'the little ponies have all come to the beach!'

Laura had a ride on one of them with her doll and when she came back she said, 'There was a little boy following behind my pony on foot.'

Then Sophie went for a ride on a pony and when she got back she said, 'There was a little boy following my pony, too.'

Andrew went up to the little boy and asked him, 'Why don't you take a ride on a pony?'

'Because I haven't got any money,' the boy replied.

'That doesn't matter,' said Andrew. 'Come and play with us. What is your name?'

'Sebastian,' said the little boy.

They built a great big sandcastle that went right up to the sky!

Well, it didn't go as high as the sky, but everybody was very happy with it, and they danced round the castle and jumped over it and sang and laughed together.

Sebastian was very happy. He was having great fun with his new friends.

When the sea washed away the sand-castle he said, 'Let's come back tomorrow and build an even bigger one.'

'What a good idea,' said Andrew.

And they did!

The little lamb was very hot, so he left his field and went down to the river.

'What fun it would be to play with the fish,' he thought.

He dabbled a hoof in the river and then . . . he fell in! The water was very cold!

He scrambled up the bank and went back to his field, to the warm sun!

Snowy Takes the Train

Snowy, the little white cat, was off on holiday. For the first time in his life, he was going to go by train.

Snowy was very impressed by the big engine at the front of the train which thundered and growled and sent up a column of smoke. His compartment was much less noisy, and he sat down on his seat next to the big window.

Just then, the guard came along in his splendid uniform with gold braid on his cap, and waved a green flag. The train started on its way, very slowly at first.

Then it began to go faster and faster.

Now and again, the engine whistled to warn everyone to get out of its way.

Soon, the song of the wheels on the rails made Snowy sleepy and he dozed off.

He woke up just in time to hear his station being called. He had arrived! Now his holiday would really begin.

163

Let's Pick Cherries

Lisa had a wonderful garden. The three cherry trees were loaded with fruit.

She climbed up a ladder which she'd placed very securely against the trunk of the first cherry tree and climbed on to the branches.

She picked lots of bright red, round, shiny cherries.

She looped a pair over her ears.

'What pretty earrings!' said Michael.

Her tame magpie came to help her pick the cherries, and the bird's sharp beak was very useful in pulling them off the tree. Of course, now and again, the magpie ate one or two!

Then the blackbird came to help them – but he ate a lot of them!

'You're a very greedy blackbird!' laughed Lisa.

Lisa went from one branch to another, very carefully, and then sat astride the biggest one to pick the rest of the cherries.

From there, she threw down all the cherries she could find to Michael, who put them in his basket.

What a wonderful harvest!

164

The Naughty Little Rabbit

Brian was putting lots of clover in the rabbit's hutch.

'Where's the little grey rabbit?' he asked.

'He's hiding,' said Jane.

'No, he isn't. That naughty little grey rabbit has got out again!'

'I think we had better look for him then,' said Jane. 'He may be lost.'

They searched for hours, but couldn't find him. And when they got back, there he was in his hutch nibbling the clover!

Jane was right. He had only been hiding!

The Singing House

David was very lucky. He lived in a house which sang all the time. It was rather odd singing, but very amusing to hear!

In the kitchen there was a little wooden clock and every quarter-hour a cuckoo popped out and shouted 'Cuckoo!'

The kitchen door squeaked when it was opened, and when it was shut.

The clock in the dining-room rang every hour and the big grandfather clock bonged away every hour as well!

But the oddest sounds came from the stairs. There were twenty steps and each step creaked or squeaked a different note – creak! crack! squeak! . . .

David thought this very amusing and he got together all the musical instruments he could find to make up an orchestra. He got a conductor's baton from the garden, selecting a nice, straight branch from a little tree. He took its leaves off and dashed back into the house.

He left the kitchen door ajar so that it squeaked all the time and then walked up and down the stairs so that they all squeaked and creaked as well! Then, he set all the clocks ringing at slightly different times.

What with the squeaking door, and the stairs, and the clocks and the cuckoo, it was quite an orchestra. But then the birds became interested by the noise so they joined in – the blackbirds and the sparrows and the finches all sang away.

Then David sang even louder to make himself heard!

A little breeze made the shutters swing back and forth and they squeaked as they did so, adding to the chorus of noises in the singing house.

When his Mother came back from shopping, she stopped outside to listen to the orchestra. It was quite good, she said, and she clapped her hands and laughed.

'But I think that is quite enough for today David,' she said.

She gave some crumbs to the birds and when they'd eaten all the crumbs they stopped singing and went to sleep in the trees in the garden.

David felt hungry and tired too. And not long after his supper he went to bed.

But tomorrow he would be up early to rehearse his orchestra again!

166

The Blue Bear

I have seen a blue bear,
A very nearly new bear,
I'd love that little blue bear
If Mummy will agree.

I could choose a brown bear,
A black bear, a Polar bear,
But I'd rather have that blue bear,
Yes, he's the one for me!

167

Tippy Loses a Present

'Oh, my goodness!' cried Tippy the little squirrel. 'I've forgotten to give Grandfather a birthday present!'

He bought a present, then went to find Grandfather squirrel's house. But he lost his way and fell into a bush.

'Oh dear!' cried Tippy, 'now I've lost Grandfather's present.'

At last, he reached Grandfather's tree.

'Tippy! How nice to see you,' said his Grandfather.

'Happy birthday, Grandfather. But, I'm sorry – I've lost your present!'

'Never mind – have a nut and some honey. It warms an old squirrel's heart to see you, with or without a present!'

Rats and Mice

Kikko the Little Donkey

Pretty John Watts,
We are troubled with rats,
Will you drive them out
of the house?
We have mice, too,
in plenty,
That feast
in the pantry;
But let them stay,
And nibble away:
What harm is a little
brown mouse?

Kikko, the little donkey at the Eiffel Tower in Paris, was feeling the heat in the hot summer. One evening, he got his stable door open and trotted off down the tree-lined avenue.

He jumped into the fountain and cooled himself down under the spray. Then he saw a lorry and jumped up into the back to take a nap.

The next morning he awoke to see that the lorry was parked in a green field. He jumped out and went skipping about in the morning mist. Then he ate some of the cool green grass.

Along a path, Kikko met a little boy pushing a barrow. His name was Henry. He was from the farm by the mill.

Henry gave the little donkey some clover.

'Here you are, little donkey – tasty clover for you!'

'Thank you,' said Kikko. 'If you like, I'll help you with your load.'

'Really? That's very nice of you – only it is a bit heavy, you know,' replied Henry.

'We'll be friends, you and I,' said Kikko happily.

And so they were, and you'll see them still at Henry's farm by the mill.

Blackberry Time

'One, two, three, off to the woods we'll go,' said Gillian, picking up her basket.

The little grey rabbit and three sparrows went with her.

'I'm going to pick some blackberries so that Mummy can make some jam,' said Gillian.

'Cheep! Cheep! said the sparrows. They knew that they would help themselves to a few blackberries from Gillian's basket.

Soon Gillian's basket was full. 'Let's go home,' she said.

'Look, Mummy,' said Gillian, 'here are lots of blackberries to make jam.'

'Oh, thank you,' said Mummy. 'You have picked a lot.'

Gillian watched as her Mummy prepared the fruit and put it into a large pan.

Soon there was a delicious smell of the blackberries cooking.

'May I taste?' asked Gillian.

'No,' said Mummy, 'you will burn your tongue. And don't go near the pan while I am out of the kitchen.'

But Gillian was a very naughty little girl. When her Mummy had gone, she climbed onto the kitchen stool and dipped a spoon into the bubbling jam to taste it.

'Oh, Mummy, Mummy, I've burnt my tongue.'

Gillian's Mummy was very, very cross with her.

When the jam had cooled, Gillian's Mummy put it into jars, and Gillian helped her to tie the paper covers.

And every time Gillian had some blackberry jam, she remembered how naughty she had been.

Diddlety, Diddlety Dumpty

Diddlety, diddlety,
dumpty,
The cat ran up the plum
tree;
Half a crown
To fetch her down,
Diddlety, diddlety,
dumpty.

172

The Sunlit Swallow

Once upon a time there was a land where the sun never shone because it didn't think the countryside was pretty enough. The trees were all stunted and never had beautiful leaves on them.

The children in the schools in that land tried to imagine what the sun looked like, and they used to draw their idea of it on the blackboard and in their school books. It was always like a big, round ball, orange in colour, or sometimes red or yellow.

One day, a swallow was on its way to the tropics and got caught in a storm. It took refuge in an old farmhouse. When the storm was over and the sun came out again, the swallow saw that its feathers were covered with raindrops, so it caught up several rays of sunlight and wound them round its body. Then, it flew off towards the tropics again.

On its way, it flew over the land where the sun never shone, and it saw the little children looking up at it in astonishment, because it was as bright as a star with all those sun's rays it had wound round itself.

The children clapped their hands with joy. So the swallow swooped down and landed on the branch of a tree. The stunted tree immediately grew and grew and was covered all over with green leaves.

Then, other swallows arrived, broke up the grey clouds in the sky and let the blue sky be seen, and with it the sun.

The children watched the sun and the blue sky and then they began to sing and dance. Soon, in what was once a grey and sunless country, all the trees sprouted beautiful green leaves and all the flowers bloomed in their marvellous colours.

The swallow had brought sunlight to the land and it would never be grey again.

173

The Little Bear

Little bear was very happy! She had found out how to climb trees.

'Not too high,' said Daddy bear.

But little bear wanted to climb higher and higher until she reached the sky and could seize the pretty, little white clouds.

Then she missed her footing and fell.

'I'll try again tomorrow,' she said. And Daddy smiled.

174

Mixed Vegetables

Ann had sown some vegetable seeds but she had lost the seed packet and had quite forgotten what they were.

Grandpa came to look at Ann's garden. 'Fine turnips you've got there,' he said.

'Er . . . yes,' said Ann.

Grandma came along one day and said, 'Those cabbages are going to be good.'

'Er . . . thank you,' said Ann.

Father came to visit Ann's garden and said, 'Those parsnips are nearly ready.'

'Er . . . I suppose they are,' said Ann.

Then Mother came along and said, 'I think those onions are big enough to eat now. Let's have some for lunch today.'

So Grandpa, Grandma and Mother and Father all came to lunch. There were no turnips, cabbages, parsnips or onions, for Ann pulled up . . . RADISHES!

'So that's what they were,' they said.

'Er . . . yes,' said Ann.

175

Some Very Strange Eggs

'Quack! Quack! Quack!'

Mrs Duck was very pleased. She was sitting on her twelve lovely eggs. Soon, there would be twelve little ducklings and they'd all go swimming along the river banks.

'Cheep! Cheep! . . .' and out they all came from their eggs – Mrs Duck was so happy. What lovely little ducklings!

'My! You are all beautiful little ducklings – but, wait a moment, you two there, you don't look like ducklings at all,' exclaimed Mrs Duck.

'We're not – we're cuckoos,' said the two little birds who'd hatched out last.

How could Mrs Duck bring up two cuckoos? What a job! But Mrs Duck decided to try, as she was a very kind duck.

When the cuckoos grew bigger, she said to them one day, 'Now you really must learn to fly, my dears.'

'We don't know how to fly, Mother Duck, but we'll try to swim like the others,' they replied.

Of course, ducklings learn to swim at once, but cuckoos can't and they would soon drown if they tried. There was only one thing to be done – Mrs Duck would have to try to carry them on her back.

And soon they were to be seen sitting on Mrs Duck's back, while the ten other little ducklings followed along behind.

The two little cuckoos found life very amusing. They played hide-and-seek most of the day, in and out of Mrs Duck's feathers.

One day, of course, they would fly, but at the moment they found life much too pleasant to bother to learn about using their wings.

176

The Little Nightingale

Little baby nightingale couldn't sing.

All the birds in the wood gave advice. The nightingale's parents listened to everything that was said to them, and they tried all the suggestions they were given, but it was no good.

'You had better go to see the wise old owl who lives in the middle of the wood,' the birds said finally.

The two nightingales took their little one to see the wise old owl. It was a very long journey.

The wise old owl had read so many books and had seen so many sick birds, he had learned so much from the stars, from the Egyptians and the Chinese, that he was very short-sighted but he still had magic in his wingtips.

He gently touched the little nightingale's brow and throat and he said, 'He'll sing, in due course.' Then he put on a compress of wild flowers and they all went home.

And one day, on the first day of summer, the little nightingale began to sing, and his beautiful voice filled the woods.

177

The Little Calf

'Edward, you've been invited to stay with your Uncle Philip during the harvest.'

'Good!' cried Edward, jumping for joy. 'I'm off to the country!'

Edward played in the tall grasses.

How wide the sky was in the country, especially during the long summer nights above the fields of waving corn!

'Poor little calf, all shut up in your stable,' said Edward. 'Come and play with me in the fields.'

Edward let him out and the little calf was overjoyed at the idea of being able to jump and play in the open. He and Edward played hide-and-seek in the waving corn, among the poppies and the daisies.

'Here I am!' cried Edward, hidden away in the grass. 'Come and find me, little calf!'

The little calf jumped here and there, and got lost in the tall cornfield.

Uncle Philip was very angry with Edward for letting the calf out, but the little calf had had a marvellous time and so had Edward!

178

The Playful Finches

While she was cleaning out the finches' cage, Frances accidentally broke one of the little windows in it. Percy, the biggest finch, poked his beak out.

He soon managed to get out altogether.

He called to Peter to come out as well. It was great fun for them – they went flying round the room, glad to be free.

Frances mended the cage and tried to get them back inside again, but it was no use – they flew all round her head, cheeping gaily.

Then, she put some birdseed on her hand and they came to her at once.

Frances quickly put them both back into their cage.

Then she put it outside in the sunlight on the terrace, where they could see everything that was going on.

179

The Scarecrow

All the animals came out of the forest.

The rabbit said, 'I'm sure I heard a cry!'

The fox said, 'I heard a call for help!'

The squirrel said, 'I heard someone crying!'

'Let's all go to see if it came from the field.'

There, in the middle of the field, a scarecrow held out its arms, all patched and torn. He said, 'I'm so ugly – nobody loves me any more!'

'Nonsense,' said the birds. 'Look, we'll make our nest in your straw hat.'

'Nonsense,' said the rabbit. 'Look, we'll make you a nice garden here, with lots of flowers in it.'

The scarecrow was very happy. He had a beautiful garden and lots of lovely flowers in it, too, and the birds came and nested in his old straw hat, where they sang all day.

180

Lin Sing

Long ago Lin Sing lived in Japan.

One morning at school, her teacher told the class, 'Tomorrow, the Emperor himself will be visiting us.'

Then the children planned what lovely gifts they could offer him. But Lin Sing's parents were very poor.

On her way home, she met an old woman who asked her why she looked so sad. When Lin Sing told her, the old woman said, 'You shall give him a gift so simple that he will repay you in plenty.'

Then the old woman told Lin Sing to go early the next day to the Snow Mountain and to fill her rice bowl with snow.

Lin Sing did so, but when she got to school, she found the snow had melted.

The Emperor arrived after a long, tiring journey. He received the splendid gifts, but he could not hide his weariness.

Then Lin Sing stepped forward, shyly, and offered him the water.

As the Emperor drank from the cool, clear water, he felt refreshed.

Then he said to Lin Sing, 'You are a wise child. In time, you will marry my son and live in the royal palace.'

So, the old woman's prophecy came true and Lin Sing lived happily ever after.

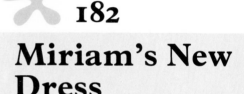

Felicity and the Stars

Felicity often sat on the porch of her house in the evenings, and watched the stars, her friends, while dreaming about them. The Great Bear fascinated her, but the Evening Star was the one she liked most of all.

One day, she was walking in the forest when it suddenly became dark, and she was quite lost.

Then, Felicity had a wonderful idea – she would follow the Evening Star, and soon she was able to see the lights of her house twinkling in the distance!

Miriam's New Dress

Miriam had worked hard at school that year. As a reward, her Mother promised her a new white dress, with little pink bows on it. Miriam was very patient during all the time spent fitting and was sure she'd be very pretty at the prize-giving. She was so excited, she could hardly wait.

The great day finally arrived.

Her Mother ironed the dress carefully and while she was doing it she heard a cry from the baby. She put down the iron at once and rushed upstairs. When she got back, the pretty pink ribbons were all badly scorched!

Miriam burst into tears.

Then fortunately her Mother had an idea – she quickly took the ribbons from the dress on Miriam's doll and stitched them on to the white dress.

'That's just what we needed, darling!' said Miriam's Mother. And the new dress looked even more beautiful than before!

183

The Big Yellow Marigold

Out in the field one day, Sylvia found a big yellow marigold with seven petals. She took them all off and threw them up into the air.

The first one fell on a lovely green beetle. Sylvia put it on her dress as a charm.

The second petal led her along the brook and she followed it till she reached the moorhens' nest. There, they laid two beautiful eggs for her.

The third petal led her to the miniature alligators' nest. These little creatures were the same size as her thumb and they lived on rose petals.

The fourth petal led her to where the miniature elephants lived. They were all white and so small that she could hold one in each hand.

The fifth petal led her to the world where the giant giraffes lived, where the grasses were as high as the trees.

The sixth petal took her to where the blue hydrangeas lived. They danced, and sang and laughed all day long.

The seventh petal showed her where the giant butterflies lived. They were as big as aeroplanes and were such lovely colours – red, and yellow, and blue, and green!

Then a big butterfly took Sylvia on her back and they returned to the field where she'd found the yellow marigold which had shown her so many wonderful sights.

184

The Little Cat

Sandra's little cat was acting very mysteriously. She didn't want to play, she ate everything that they gave her, and then she went straight back to her basket and slept all day long.

'What a lot she eats!' exclaimed Sandra. 'And she's getting so fat!'

Her Daddy smiled and said, 'Don't worry about her – she'll soon be as slim as she was before.'

And then, one fine morning, Sandra was awakened by a chorus of mews and miaous. She was surprised! Misty wasn't all alone in her basket now – there were three fluffy little kittens in there with her.

So that explained her mysterious behaviour of the last few days, and soon she was as bright and playful as ever.

185

Ella's Adventure

Ella went off to the wood with her basket to pick some blackberries.

She made her way through a forest of tall green ferns. Then she saw the little beehives in a clearing.

'Oh! Don't they look nice!' she exclaimed. She went a little closer and watched the bees flying in and out with their loads of pollen.

'Ah, ha!' said a growly voice behind her. 'You're just the person I need to help me get this honey into my pots.'

Ella saw a big brown bear just behind her and she felt rather scared of him.

But he was a very friendly brown bear, and when she had finished helping him he gave her three large pots of honey to take home for tea.

'Oh, thank you,' said Ella. 'Mummy will be pleased.'

186

The Giraffe

A giraffe with looks so appealing,
Poked his head through a very high
*   ceiling.*
Looking round him he saw
Woollen socks on the floor,
Which he ate without sorrow or feeling!

Golden Ear's Voyage

In the farmyard there were ducks, and geese, and pigs, and sheep, and the big draught horse, and there was Golden Ear, the little horse.

One summer night when the moon was full and shining brightly, Golden Ear decided to go on a voyage.

He galloped away across the fields and the plains, and he arrived in a country where only thistles grew in the fields. He didn't like thistles.

The sun was very hot. Shortly, a donkey came along and he said to Golden Ear, 'There's a river not very far from here where you can drink.'

They journeyed along together in the stifling heat. Golden Ear didn't feel very well, but he drank lots of water. In fact, he drank rather too much and he fell sick with fever. He lay down under a palm tree. He would so like to see all his friends in the farmyard again!

Along came a small boy with a mule. The donkey told them about Golden Ear falling ill.

The boy gave the little horse some tablets and he felt better at once. He slept soundly all night.

The next day Golden Ear, the little boy and the mule, and the donkey all left for the farm together.

They arrived late in the evening and all the animals were overjoyed to see them. The little boy and the mule stayed with them, and so did the little grey donkey.

Golden Ear would never leave his beloved farm again. The world was much too big a place for him!

188

Where is Little Fox?

Martin called from the field, 'Come and look at the little fox I've found!'

All the boys in the holiday camp went to see it. And Martin took it back to the camp.

Martin soon became the little fox's best friend, and one night the little fox came and snuggled up to him on his bed.

'I'm sure he likes me,' said Martin.

Then, one day, the little fox disappeared. Everyone searched for him, in the fields, the woods and on the mountains. They searched for hours.

But they didn't find him, and in their little tents that night the children felt very sad.

Then, suddenly, Martin cried, 'Here he is! The little fox was sleeping in my bed!'

All the children went to look, overjoyed that little fox had come back to them.

189

Frog Number Ten

Mother frog was very happy with her ten little green frogs, all swimming about.

'Come along, jump into the pond, frog number ten,' said his Mother.

But frog number ten was rather scared of jumping.

'Look at your little brothers and sisters!' cried his Mother, 'and the ducks, too. They all jump. Try jumping from the waterlily leaf there.'

Frog number ten screwed up his courage and jumped. Splosh!

'Look, Mummy,' he cried. 'I'll jump again now. Jumping is fun!'

190

Misty Escapes

Florence and Caroline were off on their holidays.

'We can't take the cat camping with us,' said Mummy.

So, the children gave the cat to their Aunt.

But Misty, the cat, escaped and Aunt put a note on her front door: Lost – small marmalade cat.

Soon, there was a knock at the door.

'Come in!' said Aunt.

'We've found your cat,' said a little boy.

'Thank you, my boy,' said Aunt. 'Wait a moment – here are three biscuits for you.'

The very next day, Misty escaped again, but soon there was a knock at the door.

'Come in!' said Aunt.

'We've found your cat,' said a group of children.

'Thank you very much, children,' said Aunt. 'As a reward, I'm going to give you some biscuits.'

At last, the holiday caravan returned.

'Ah!' said Aunt, 'at last I'm going to get some peace and the marmalade cat can go back to its proper home!'

191
Pip, the Elf in the Valley

Pip the elf was very useful in entertaining sick children in the valley. One evening, he heard little Luke calling for him and went to see him.

'What's the matter with you, Luke, and what can I do for you?' asked Pip.

'Oh, Pip, I've got a temperature and a headache and I'm so bored with being in bed. What can I do? – show me something to do!' said Luke.

'Why are you bored? There are lots of things to amuse you,' said Pip.

'What things?' asked Luke in surprise.

'Look! There – above you – the stars, flashing like diamonds. Do you know that there are millions of stars, far, far away from us on Earth? And look, that moth, flying round your light. Did you know it was once just a little caterpillar, then it became a larva asleep in a cocoon, until it emerged as a beautiful moth in the lamplight? And the bees, have you never asked yourself how they are born, and how they live?'

'The stars, the moth, the bees, they all sound so interesting. Tell me stories about them, Pip!' cried Luke.

And while Pip told stories about them, Luke listened and bit by bit, his temperature went down, his headache vanished and his boredom went too. He dreamed about Pip's stories of animals and stars.

Pip blew softly and the lamp went out. He then blew gently again and Luke's eyes closed in sleep. Pip flew off to see another little child who was ill in bed.

192

Bridget and the Butterfly

Bridget went to the fields where the geese were feeding under the watchful eye of Jerry, their little shepherd, and she sat down beside him.

Suddenly, she saw a beautiful red and yellow butterfly coming towards her. The butterfly didn't seem at all wild. It perched on the little girl's hair, like a beautiful bow. Then it came and perched on her shoulder.

Then, it flew away, and Bridget ran after it. The butterfly crossed the field, and then went along the river bank, while Bridget ran alongside, fascinated by the little river's songs and lovely blue water.

She was very hot, so she washed her face and hands in the cool water, while the butterfly sucked nectar from a beautiful flower on the bank.

Bridget had such fun with the butterfly, running after it over lots of fields and discovering all sorts of different flowers and insects, that she was quite surprised to hear the bell go for twelve o'clock. Time for lunch!

But after lunch was over, she found her friend the butterfly waiting for her in the field and the two of them began to play again.

And during all that holiday the butterfly was Bridget's best friend.

193

Floppy, the Donkey

Floppy was a little grey donkey who was all alone in a big field of red clover.

'Where are you going, little train?' he asked.

'I'm off to the city,' said the train.

'What luck you've got,' said Floppy.

'Come with me if you want to,' said the train.

Floppy jumped on to a waggon full of boxes.

When they got to the city, Floppy jumped out on to the platform.

But the railway guard caught him and he was locked up in a dark, narrow stable.

How bitterly he regretted leaving his dear field.

He bit through his rope and jumped over the stable door.

He got to the station just in time.

'Please take me back, little train,' he said. 'I hate the big city.'

And soon Floppy was home again.

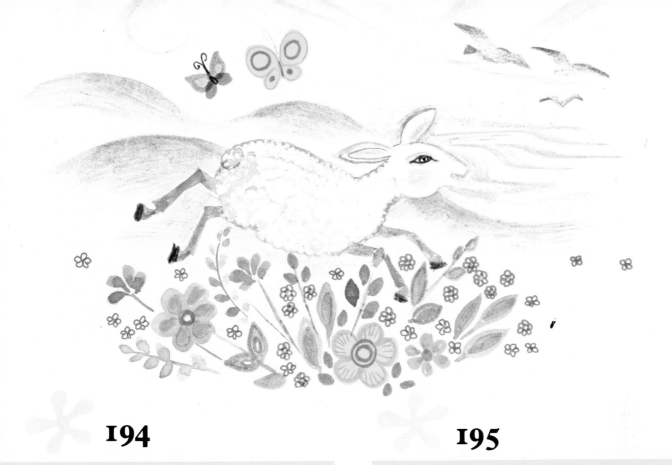

194

Sea Treasure

195

Frisky's Adventure

Once there was a beautiful seashell that belonged to the Queen of the Sea Fairies.

One night, in a terrible storm, the sea swept the little shell from the ocean palace and carried it miles away.

When at last the storm was over, the little shell found it was near land and the waves gently washed it on to a warm sandy beach.

In time a small boy came by. He picked up the little shell and held it to his ear.

Music! The little shell sang him a song the Sea Fairies had once sung.

Then the little boy took his sea treasure home and the little shell was happy.

Frisky the little lamb was feeling very restless. He was tired of the same green field day after day.

He had heard tales of a beautiful field near the sea that was carpeted with flowers, and he longed to see it.

'I'll visit that flowery field,' Frisky decided. 'I know where it is.'

And so off he set.

When he got there . . . what a wonderful surprise! It was better than he had imagined. There were so many flowers and of so many colours.

He hopped and skipped about, danced with the lively butterflies that were there, had a dip in the sea, and raced with the seagulls.

When it was time to go home Frisky said goodbye to the flowers, the butterflies, the sea and the seagulls, and promised to visit them again soon.

 **196**

Hoop-La

Sally and her Mother had arrived at the Pennydown Fete. There were stalls and sideshows of every kind but Sally liked the hoop-la stall best.

'Three hoops for three pence,' called the man at the stall.

Sally counted three new pence from her purse and gave the money to the man. He gave her three little hoops and one more . . . just for luck.

Sally threw the first hoop. It sailed over the stall to the other side. The next one hooked itself on to a post and the third one landed on a man's head!

'One more,' said a little boy called Joe, who had been watching. 'Would you like me to try?'

'Oh, thank you,' said Sally.

The little boy took the last hoop, closed one eye and took careful aim. The hoop went spinning and landed . . . right over a beautiful rag doll!

'Bravo!' shrieked Sally, delightedly.

'Now Joe deserves a prize,' said Sally's Mother. So they went to the stall selling home-made cakes and bought a raspberry bun for Sally and a cream bun for Joe, the hoop-la champion!

197

Donkey, Donkey

*Donkey, donkey, old and
 grey,
Open your mouth and
 gently bray;
Lift your ears and blow
 your horn,
To wake the world this
 sleepy morn.*

198

Practical Jokers!

Mathew and Jocelyn were two pranksters. They were always playing practical jokes and not always in the best of taste.

When the telephone rang, they would answer, 'Fire Brigade here . . .' or 'Mummy's out . . .' when she was in the kitchen, and things like that.

One fine day a voice on the telephone said, 'You two have won first prize in our draw – one has got a toy train and the other a bicycle. Go to the end of the village by the hill to collect your prizes!'

Despite the heat that day, the two children set off at once and they walked miles.

Of course, when they got to the end of the village by the hill, there wasn't anyone there – and no prizes either!

They walked slowly back home again.

'You see, it's not always the same people who play tricks,' said their Mother. 'Sometimes, other people play tricks on you and that's how you learn to be good losers!'

199

The Garden After Rain

A huge black cloud threw a shadow over the bright day, and soon a summer storm was lashing Jeremy's garden with rain. There were puddles everywhere.

'What luck,' said the little green frogs. 'We were praying for rain.'

But the birds took shelter. The flowers weren't happy and the honeybee which was sheltering inside the red rose still got wet.

'Buzz! Buzz!' it said, as it shook its wings and flew slowly back to its hive.

The eagle went up to the great black cloud and asked it to move away elsewhere, and the cloud obliged. It was rather flattered by the eagle's attention.

Then came the rainbow. It shone in the puddles where the little green frogs were splashing and dancing about.

Then out came the laughing sun again and the flowers shook off the raindrops in brilliant flashes of colour. The honeybee returned to the garden and the birds chirped happily in the trees.

200

The Starry Sky

Kikko, the little squirrel, had a bad cold and was confined to his bed.

Mother Squirrel looked after him with great care. She tucked the warm blankets round him and asked him if there was anything he wanted.

'I would like to see a sky full of stars!' he said.

Now, how could she do that for him?

He wasn't allowed out of bed. He couldn't even go outside their nest in the tall tree.

But one warm summer night, all his little friends came along and said, 'Let's go outside and see the starry sky. But we musn't stay out too long.'

'What a wonderful sight!' exclaimed Kikko. And he felt better already.

201

Old Mother Hubbard

Old Mother Hubbard
Went to the cupboard
To fetch her poor dog a bone;
But when she got there
The cupboard was bare,
And so the poor dog had none.

She went to the fruiterer's
To buy him some fruit;
But when she came back
He was playing the flute.

She went to the hatter's
To buy him a hat;
But when she came back
He was feeding the cat.

She went to the tailor's
To buy him a coat;
But when she came back
He was riding a goat.

The dame made a curtsy,
The dog made a bow;
The dame said, 'Your servant,'
The dog said, 'Bow-wow.'

202

Old Mrs Jampot

All the children knew old Mrs Jampot and they all liked her very much.

She lived on the edge of the forest in a little house surrounded by flowers.

Each summer, the children went to see her and helped to clean out the pots she cooked the jams in, and they were allowed to eat some of the strawberries and raspberries and gooseberries, and the blackberries and apricots.

But one day old Mrs Jampot got rheumatism and she couldn't manage to prepare the fruit for the jam.

The children all went to help her.

'Let us help you,' they said. 'We'll wash the fruit and stone the apricots for you Mrs Jampot.'

Old Mrs Jampot smiled at them all and thought what a good thing it was jam she made.

203
The Jealous Sparrow

Giles found a little blackbird which had fallen out of its nest, and he took it home.

Jane clapped her hands with joy, but Jasper the tame sparrow was jealous.

'He's not going to like another little bird in the same house!' laughed Mummy.

And he wasn't – he scattered the rice in a bowl on the table as he flew in and out of the window, just to show that he didn't approve of the little blackbird sharing the house and garden with him!

The little blackbird was very frightened at first, but he soon settled down and became one of the family.

He and Jasper became firm friends, and the two birds were soon flying down from the tree outside to eat from the outstretched hands of Giles and Jane as they sat on the terrace.

204

Brave Father Wolf

'Look-out!' cried Father wolf. 'Here come the hunting dogs!' Mother wolf and her cubs got ready to run.

'I'll make the dogs run after me towards the river,' said Father wolf. 'You take the cubs the other way through the woods!'

Mother wolf and the cubs ran as fast as they could into the woods, while the wolf ran across the field in view of the dogs.

They raced after him, barking savagely, getting closer and closer.

Then, suddenly, the wolf reached the river bank and plunged into the water, swimming for the opposite bank.

The dogs lost his scent at the river's edge and gave up the chase.

In their den, Mother wolf and the cubs waited anxiously for their Father.

Then, with a great leap, he was there, and the family was safely together again.

205

A Little Prayer

On Sundays when the church bells ring
I sit outside and quietly sing
My little hymns to God and pray
My little prayers. I mostly say:
'Thank you, God, for a lovely day!'

206

Stephanie and the Rabbits

On a very hot day in summer, Stephanie went into the forest to play with her ball.

Suddenly, the ball rolled away and fell into the river.

She tried to get it back but it floated further away. Then she saw a little boat by the river bank and she got into it and rowed towards the ball. She fished it out of the water and as she did so, a frog jumped into the boat with her.

Then she saw an island, with trees and grasses and rabbits on it.

They were white rabbits, with one or two russet-coloured ones, and all were very tame. Stephanie shook their paws in greeting, and the frog did the same.

She found some carrots, some black-berries and some ducks' eggs and they all sat down to eat lunch.

The rabbits made up a bed of leaves for her and she lay down to sleep.

The next morning, she and the little frog went off in the boat together and they said goodbye to their new friends, the rabbits, but they promised to come back again one day.

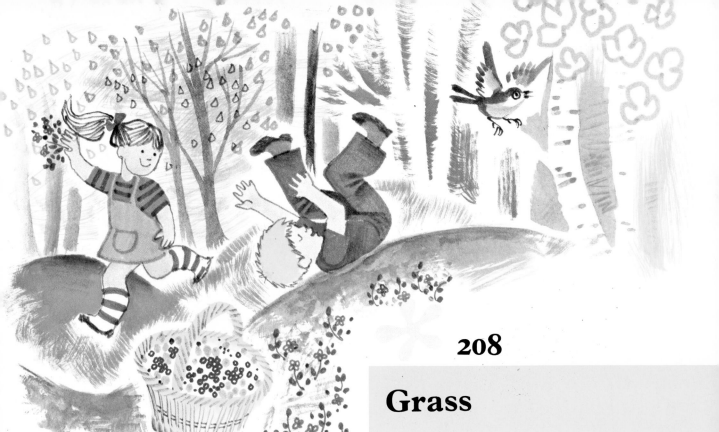

208

Grass

I love grass –
Lots and lots of grass;
I just can't pass
When I see grass!
I have to stop
And roll and hop,
And kneel and flop
When I see grass!

207

Picking Blackberries

'Come and pick blackberries with me,' said Grandfather to John and Cathy, 'but mind you stay close to me while we're out in the woods.'

It was such fun running about in the woods, and rolling about on the soft, green moss!

Then the basket was full of blackberries at last and Grandfather called, 'John! Cathy! Come along – time to go home!'

He searched here and there.

'Ah! I know where they are – they've gone to hide in the hollow by the glade!' he said.

Then Cathy and John appeared and said, 'Ah, there you are, Grandfather – we've been searching for you for hours!'

'What cheek!' laughed Grandfather.

209

Who Knows?

Who knows, who knows
Where the wolf goes.
And what does he do all day?

Does he . . .
Talk to the flowers
For hours and hours,
Or
Chase after leaves
That fall from the trees,
Or
Crouch in the grass
Where grey rabbits pass,
Or
Sleep in the sun
When hunting is done.

Who knows, who knows
Where the wolf goes.
What does he do all day?

210

Over the Hills

Over the hills
And far away,
I kick my heels,
I frolic and play,
For I am chasing
The wind today,
Over the hills
And far away.

Harvey the Urchin

Edgar lived in a fine house with a big garden filled with flowers and fruit trees.

One evening, he heard a noise in the garden. At first, he thought it must be a cat in the shrubbery and he went to look.

But it wasn't a cat – it was Harvey, a little boy who lived in the village, and all his clothes were patched and worn. He was what Edgar's father called an urchin.

Edgar said to him, 'I know what you're up to – you're stealing the peaches!'

Harvey was angry at being caught in the very act of doing just that, and he replied, 'Well, I don't care – it isn't right that some people should have everything and others nothing!'

Edgar thought this was reasonable and said, 'You're quite right! Here, I'll help you pick some roses for your Mother!'

Harvey was very surprised – then, suddenly, he held out his hand. 'Will you be my friend?' he said to Edgar.

'Of course I will be,' said Edgar. 'And you must come to the garden to play whenever you wish.'

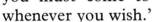

212

Come for a Swim

*Won't you come
And have a swim?
I'm as happy as can be!
Won't you come
And have a splash?
The fish invited me.*

*Won't you come
And join the fun?
It's warm as warm can be.*

213

Beatrice Becomes a Nurse

'Cheep! Cheep!' called the sparrows. They were all flying about in great dismay.

One of them had broken a wing.

Beatrice went out into the garden at once to see what she could do. She put a tiny piece of matchwood under the wing and bound it up gently.

Beatrice looked after the little sparrow for several days and then let it out into the garden, where it could hop about.

'Cheep!' said the sparrow in gratitude.

'I'll bring you some crumbs,' said Beatrice.

'Cheep! Cheep! Cheep!' called the happy sparrow.

214

The Picnic

In the long meadow, the field-mice family were getting ready for a picnic. Mrs Fieldmouse had baked some delicious corn pancakes that morning and had packed them all neatly in a hamper. Then she put in some slices of cheesecake, a jug of dandelion wine and last of all, a pot of her special clover honey.

Just as they were setting off, Pussycat Purrkins came along, chasing a butterfly. He was so busy trying to catch the gentle creature that he didn't see the little mice – but they saw Pussycat Purrkins!

They ran as hard as they could through the long grass until they came to a little clearing where pink and white daisies grew. It was the perfect place for a picnic and they soon forgot all about Pussycat Purrkins.

The little fieldmice settled down to enjoy themselves. After lunch, Mr Fieldmouse found an old sock in the grass – just the thing to curl up in for a nap. But, not for long . . .

Two furry ears appeared over a clump of grass. Then two bright green eyes, followed by one very pink nose and then, all of . . . Pussycat Purrkins.

How those poor little mice scattered and scampered.

Pussycat Purrkins soon gave up the chase. He had found Mrs Fieldmouse's special pot of clover honey, which he lapped to the very last lick!

215

The Little Boat

On a beautiful stream, a little wooden boat was fast asleep.

It awoke and knew that it wanted to go on a long journey.

The eagle used its powerful beak to cut the rope that tied the little boat to the jetty.

'There you are, little boat – you're free!' said the eagle, 'and bon voyage!'

All the birds sat inside the little boat, while the rabbits and moles and squirrels came down to the shore to see it off.

'The little boat is going on a journey with the birds – we ought to go too!' they all said to each other.

So they all climbed into the boat as well and the boat set off.

They soon arrived in a wonderful land where there were thousands of tulips of every colour and lots of red squirrels.

It so happened that the day they arrived was the day of the tulips' Ball!

'It will be fun!' said a rabbit to a robin.

They danced, and sang and had a marvellous time. The birds all had too much tulip juice and felt very sleepy afterwards.

'I'm staying here,' said the little boat, 'when the tulips' Ball is over. It's such a lovely place!'

216
Luke Goes on Holiday

Luke was on holiday at the seaside. On the first day he built a sandcastle. Then his dog, Boffin, dug a hole and the sandcastle fell into it!

The next day, Luke said to Boffin, 'You dig a hole first, then I'll build my sandcastle around it.'

So that is what they did. When it was finished, Luke said, 'Now we need some water for the hole, for the castle pond.'

Luke fetched his bucket and they both ran to the edge of the sea. Luke had to fill his bucket several times before the hole was full, for Boffin had dug a very deep one!

Just as Luke was dipping his bucket into the sea for the last time, a little fish popped out and landed in the bucket. Luke was delighted. Now his castle had a proper pond with a real fish in it!

217
Peter and the Butterfly

Little green frog was Peter's special friend. They were both sunbathing in the garden one day when a beautiful red and black butterfly came and sat on a yellow rose.

'I'm going to catch it,' said Peter to his friend the frog.

He crept up to the butterfly very slowly, with his butterfly net all ready. The butterfly didn't move and little Peter thought it was going to be easy to catch it. But just as his net was a few inches away, the butterfly decided to fly away!

'Croak! Croak!' said the frog. 'You missed it!'

So Peter went towards the butterfly again, this time even more slowly and carefully. The butterfly smiled to itself – of course it knew what little Peter was trying to do, so it waited till the boy was almost up to it, then it flew away again!

'It doesn't want to be put in a case!' croaked the frog. 'But if you let it alone now, it will come to you!'

So little Peter sat down on the edge of the pond where his little friend the frog lived, and there they waited.

The butterfly came back no longer afraid. It settled gently on top of little Peter's head and then on his shoulder.

Peter was very pleased because he had found a new friend.

218

Chickee the Canary

One hot summer's day in his cage, Chickee the canary was feeling bored. He was very hot and he'd have loved to get out and go and swim with the ducks in their pond.

Lucy opened the door of his cage to feed him.

In a flash, he had got out of the cage.

And a few moments later, there he was in the duck pond, splash, splosh!

But then he discovered that he couldn't swim. What was he to do now? Help!

'Quack! Quack!' called old Mrs Duck.

She swam across the pond and pulled the wet canary out of the water. He was cold and miserable.

Lucy then came running along. She dried her pet canary gently with a soft handkerchief and fed him with some seed from her hand.

Chickee had had a bad fright. He wouldn't go near the duck pond again!

A New Friend

Minny was a very small cat who had been abandoned, and she was very sad.

Paul was a little boy who would not be able to go away on holiday.

'Why don't you come and play with me?' Paul asked Minny. 'I'd like us to be friends.'

That evening, with Minny held safely in his arms, he took the cat to his room.

Now, the little boy was no longer alone – he had Minny to keep him company. Paul gave him an old basket and a red cushion he'd found in the loft.

Minny was very pleased. She purred with pleasure and settled down in the basket on top of the cushion.

Paul was very pleased too. If he had gone on holiday he would never have met his new friend, Minny the cat!

James and the Pigeon

Far away, in the huge forests of West Africa, there lived a little boy called James.

Each morning, he washed himself in the river. He sang as he collected bananas for breakfast and pineapples for their juice. It was good to drink when he was thirsty.

James's Mother pounded millet in a large pot and she cooked some bananas over a fire.

James went off to pick some mangoes and dates.

One day, he found a pigeon which had been wounded by a hunter.

James picked it up and brought it back to their camp where he asked a medicine man to heal its wound.

The medicine man took care of the pigeon and after a few weeks it was well enough for James to set it free.

221

The Elephant Who Had No Tusks

Jerry was a very unhappy elephant – he didn't have any lovely ivory tusks!

All the other elephants made fun of him!

Jerry was so unhappy that one day he left the herd altogether.

That night, he slept under the stars and the yellow moon. While he was asleep, a great leopard came and tried to attack him, but fortunately he was warned of the danger just in time by a vulture.

One day, some white hunters caught him in a big net and they took him away to a special reserve in the middle of Africa.

All the animals there lived in peace and were very happy and they thought Jerry was the nicest little elephant they had ever seen.

* **222**

* **223**

The Rusty Bike

Today

'Here, come and look!' cried Raymond.
'I've found an old bike!'

His four friends crowded round the
bicycle.

'It's not exactly new,' they said. 'It's
all rusty!'

'It's all bent, too, and it probably won't
even run!'

'We'll get to work,' said Raymond, 'and
we'll make it a new bike again!'

'I've got some paint here,' said Mark.

'I'll paint it,' said Raymond.

They both had a go at painting it
bright red.

The rusty old bike now looked as good
as new.

'Who'll try it out first?' asked Raymond.

'Me! Me!' they all cried.

And after that the old bike was brought
out every summer's evening and every
school holiday and was never allowed to
get rusty again.

As I was going along my way,
I met a wolf and chanced to say,
'How is the world with you today?
Pray, how is your world today?'

He looked at me once, then just to be sure,
He looked at me twice and offered his paw.
'Today is the same as it was before,
It's just the same as before.'

 **224**

The Japanese Fish

There was once a little Japanese fish all alone in his fishbowl. His little brothers had been sold.

But one summer morning, Christopher bought him.

When they got home, Christopher put him in a nice big fishbowl and he said, 'I shall call you Jim.'

Life became much more interesting. Jim liked Christopher very much.

Then Christopher bought a goldfish, which he called Joe.

One day while Christopher's Mother was changing the water in the fishbowl, Joe started leaping about. And he leapt right out of the bowl, pulling Jim along with him!

Out of water altogether, both Jim and Joe felt quite lost.

Luckily, Christopher's kitten mewed so loudly that Christopher's Mother came back to see what had happened, and she put both fish back into their bowl again.

As a reward that evening, Christopher gave some juicy sardines to his kitten for saving the fish's lives.

Jim swam round and round inside the bowl to show how pleased he was, and Joe promised not to be so silly in future.

225

A Difficult Little Boy

Gilbert was a little boy who was rather difficult. When he got into a temper, which was often, he would yell and kick at anything near him. His Mother didn't know what to do with him!

'What will happen to him when he gets older if he goes on like this?' she thought in despair.

One day, his parents were invited to stay with some friends at the seaside. Gilbert was very happy when he heard this – there would be swimming, and the beach, and games, and friends to see!

Now, on the first day of their holiday, Gilbert flew into a temper and his parents could not calm him. But their friends' little boy said to Gilbert, 'There's no need to be cross. Why don't we go and play on the beach?'

As they walked off along the sand, Gilbert felt very ashamed, and he decided that he was going to enjoy his holiday.

226

Pippo and His Friends

Pippo was a little white dog, with curly hair like a lamb's coat. One fine day in summer he was running after a little green frog and he ran so far he got lost.

Then, an old caravan pulled up near him and someone said, 'Oh! Look, a little lost dog!'

Oliver and Bella, the two children in the caravan, picked Pippo up and said to their Mother, 'Look, we've found a little lost dog – and he's very hungry!'

After searching for his owner and not finding anyone, the children's parents said they could keep him.

Pippo was very happy, and after eating a large juicy bone, he went to sleep.

227

Tibbles and Greypoke

Tibbles the cat and Greypoke the little donkey were off on their holidays.

Greypoke was getting tired and he was glad to see a sign by the road which said: To the seaside. He was going to see Grandfather Greypoke.

A cat with a funny accent told them where to go and soon they were at Greypoke's Grandfather's house.

The old donkey led them all to the beach. Tibbles and Greypoke had never seen so much water, and Greypoke ran about along the beach splashing his hooves in the sea.

That day, Tibbles and Greypoke were too timid to splash in the water. But they liked it so much the next day, that they made plans to stay on holiday longer.

228

The Procession

Frank and Valerie were on holiday with their favourite Aunt. As it was Sunday the whole village turned out for the procession to the church, and all the children were dressed in their best clothes.

Mabby the cat didn't seem at all well that day and he sat by the window watching as the procession started, mewing. Frank and Valerie could not understand what was wrong with him, but their Aunt said, 'He wants to be in the procession too.'

'Well,' said Valerie, 'let's take him along.' She tied a bow around his neck, and off they went to join in the fun!

229

The Shark

It was summer. Deep down in the sea the little fish was swimming about tirelessly. His Grandmother was very old and she sat down on a rock and said to him, 'You go off and swim round a bit more while I rest here – but be careful of the shark!'

The little fish said he wasn't afraid of sharks.

He swam down among the seaweeds and accidentally bumped into the sea anemone.

'Silly fish!' said the anemone crossly. 'Why don't you look where you're going!'

The little fish then saw a whale, who said, 'Look out for the shark!'

'I'm not afraid of him,' replied the little fish. 'If I see him, I'll lead him a dance!'

And just as he spoke, along came the shark. He raced through the water, snapping at every fish in his way. The little fish swam away as fast as he could, but the shark was close behind.

The grumpy old sea anemone refused to hide the little fish, but the kind octopus gave him time to escape by throwing one of his tentacles around the shark.

The little fish swam away thankfully, vowing to listen to Grandmother in future.

Little Hameed

Little Hameed was on his way back from the market, where he had bought a camel.

The camel said he wanted to go free, so Hameed let him off his string.

The camel was very happy and he ran towards an oasis on the horizon – but unfortunately it was only a mirage, there wasn't an oasis there.

So Hameed gave him some cool, fresh water from a big canvas sack he had.

Two jackals passed and wished them 'Good day!'

They seemed rather jealous, as they were friends of little Hameed.

'We'll all play games together,' Hameed promised the two jackals and the camel, and everybody was happy again.

They all travelled to the oasis where they rested in the shade of the palm trees.

Cartwheels

It was summertime. Elizabeth was turning cartwheels on the grass.

The frogs thought she was very clever and asked her to show them how she did it.

The little pink piglet also wanted to turn cartwheels, but he fell over and got a large lump on his head!

The frogs did very well, but the old brown cow was no good at all – she tried four times, and fell over each time! Everybody laughed at her.

The old sheep and her little lamb tried their best, but they weren't very good at it.

Then the donkeys tried it.

Elizabeth was having such fun!

And lastly, the young foal tried, but it wasn't as good at turning cartwheels as it was at galloping!

The animals had had great fun, but they decided Elizabeth was much better at turning cartwheels than they were!

232

Laurence the Lion

Laurence the lion loved water-skiing. Every holiday, he packed his caravan and climbed into his smart red sports car and drove to the seaside.

One holiday, Laurence went to a part of the coast he had never been to before. The sea certainly looked blue and just right for water-skiing.

Laurence unpacked his things, put on his swimming shorts and carried his water-skis down to the beach. 'All I need now is a boat to tow me,' he said.

A boy in a fast speed-boat skimmed by.

'Hey, wait for me!' cried Laurence.

The boy in the speed-boat came back. 'I've never towed a lion on skis before,' he said. 'Here's a tow-line. Hold tight!'

Laurence hung on and away they went.

'Once round that buoy and back again,' shouted Laurence. But the buoy wasn't a buoy at all – it was a friendly dolphin!

Laurence was so surprised when the dolphin popped his head out of the sea, that he fell into the water – SPLASH!

He didn't have to worry. The playful dolphin carried him safely back to the beach. What fun! It was going to be Laurence's best holiday ever!

233

The Sandcastle

Sylvia and Nathalie were on holiday in a little fishing village. Every day they went down to the beach and they tried to build bigger sandcastles than the previous day. They decorated them with lovely seashells and green and blue seaweed.

But there was one nasty boy who would always come along when they had finished their castle and jump on it with both feet.

One day, he didn't appear.

The two little girls heard later that he had fallen and hurt his foot while jumping on someone else's sandcastle.

'Serve him right!' they said. 'He won't do it again!'

234

The Swallow's Song

Goodbye, children,
I must go
To warmer lands
Before the snow
Comes tumbling down
And makes me freeze
And hides the grass
And flowers and trees.
But I'll be back
The first warm day
Of summer time –
To flit and play.

235

If I Could

I would, if I could,
If I couldn't, how could I?
I couldn't, without I
could, could I?
Could you, without you
could, could ye?
Could ye? Could ye?
Could you, without you
could, could ye?

236

The Little Jackal

Deep in the forest there lived a little jackal. He was very gentle.

One evening, he was walking along the banks of the river when he met a pink flamingo.

This greedy bird had just swallowed three fish very quickly, and was choking on his meal.

The little jackal took a stick and pushed the fish down the flamingo's throat.

The flamingo thanked the jackal and flew away.

John arrived on the scene. He wasn't feeling very happy as he hadn't caught many fish for his supper.

The little jackal called to the flamingo to go and get some fish for John.

And very soon, the little black boy's basket was full.

John thanked the little jackal and the flamingo.

He walked back home to his round hut in the village, accompanied by monkeys and his friend the warthog, and they all had a splendid meal of sweet potatoes.

237

Leap-Lamb!

'Baa! Baa!' cried Joe, the youngest lamb in Alice's flock of sheep. 'Let's play leap-lamb instead of leap-frog!'

'What a good idea!' said Alice. She got down on all fours and Joe the lamb leaped over her.

But he fell over – bump! – on to his back and he was very upset!

Alice laughed and said, 'I'll show you how to do it!'

She jumped over Joe's back without falling down, and then Joe tried again.

But it was no good – he fell over again!

He was very upset and cried.

'You're too small for that game,' said Mickey the squirrel. Next year, you'll be big enough to do it without falling over.'

So Joe the lamb had to make do with running races with Alice and her pet squirrel.

Of course, it was much easier to run races, and Joe the lamb was quite good at it. In fact he was better than Alice!

238

Bamboula

Bamboula went to market very early.

At the market there were lots of people, and he got pushed this way and that and nearly deafened by the noise.

He bought some rice, some dried fish, some eggs, a bunch of bananas and some bright red cotton for his Mother.

His pet monkey, Jungo, helped him, but the cunning monkey ate two bananas when Bamboula wasn't looking!

Bousso, Bamboula's friend, suggested that they all travel home on the back of his little grey donkey. But Jungo didn't like being on the donkey's back and he made all sorts of funny faces!

When they got home, Bamboula's Mother was very pleased with what he had bought and gave him a honey cake.

Jilly the Doll

Florence had gone on holiday and quite forgotten about Jilly her doll. She had been playing with her and had left her outside in the grass.

Night came and Jilly shivered in the cold. She began to cry.

The glow-worm said, 'Close your eyes and go to sleep!'

The next morning, Jilly played with the little lambs. But when the evening came, they all went indoors to their Mother.

Jilly was left alone outside and she was frightened.

'Don't worry!' said the sheep. 'Come and look – I've got you some milk, all creamy and warm.'

The lambs crowded round her to keep her warm.

Then she heard a voice say, 'Hello Jilly – I'm the farm dog. Climb on my back and I'll take you inside.'

Soon she was back with Florence.

'There you are, Jilly, how glad I am to see you again!'

The Bear and the Stars

Bobby, the little bear, wanted to pick the stars from the sky.

He climbed up a tree, right to the top, but the stars were still far away.

Then he looked down into the lake below him and saw . . . the STARS!

He dived from the top of the tree into the lake to pick them from the water – but all he could find was a stone!

'What a silly bear he is!' said the frogs.

✳ 241

What a Wonderful Day!

'It really is too bad!' said the grey horse. 'Our masters go off to the seaside and leave us here to work!'

'We have to stay behind to look after the house!' said the donkey.

'Come along,' said the cow. 'We'll go to the seaside as well!'

The horse, the donkey and the cow left for the seaside and walked along the hot, dusty road that led to the sea.

What fun they all had on the beach, after such a long journey. The donkey went fishing for crabs. The red cow found a basketful of mussels. And the grey horse went after shrimps with a net.

What a wonderful day!

✳ 242

The Little Owl

Every evening, the little owl came to say goodnight to Dominic.

But this evening, she didn't come, and Dominic began to get worried.

Then, suddenly, little owl flew in through the open window. She had been injured.

Dominic quickly cleaned the wound.

'Thank you, little owl, for coming to see me,' he said.

'Tu-whit, tu-whoo!' she replied.

She flew up on to the head of his bed, and perched there for the night. She would soon be much better.

'Goodnight!' said Dominic. He knew he was lucky to have such a friend.

✱ 243

Summer is the Best Season

'When summer comes,' said Susie, who was rather greedy, 'Mummy makes lots of jam – apricot and plum, mostly. I put on a big apron, and help her to weigh the lovely ripe fruit while the sticky juice runs through my fingers!'

'When summer comes,' said Peter, 'Grandfather and I leave early in the morning to go fishing. It's nice and cool under the big trees along the river bank. I can watch the silver fish darting about in the waving river grasses. Sometimes, one of them gets caught on my fishing hook, but I always put him back in the river.

'Sometimes, too, we spend a whole day on the farm. With my friend John we take the sheep up to the pastures, and while they crop the grass we might build a sort of log cabin with tree branches, or perhaps we build a dam to divert the course of the little stream.'

Summer is the best season of the year.

✱ 244

A Silly Quarrel

Molly, my sister, and I fell out,
And what do you think it was all about?
She loved coffee and I loved tea,
And that was the reason we couldn't agree.

246
Nutty the Fieldmouse

'Letter for you,' said Mr Shrew, the postman, to Nutty's Mother one morning.

'Oh dear!' said Nutty's Mother, reading the letter, 'it's from cousin Tom in the town – he's not well – I shall have to go to see him today.'

'I'll be good while you're away, Mummy,' promised Nutty.

As soon as his Mother had gone, he went out to play with his friend Blue Butterfly.

The butterfly made him some wings out of tissue paper, and tied them round the little fieldmouse. Nutty tried flying in them, but he crashed and got a bump on his head for his pains.

The skylark sang that it was twelve noon and time for lunch, so Nutty said goodbye to Blue Butterfly.

On the way home he met grey rabbit. She took him up on to her back and they fairly flew along, and arrived just in time for lunch.

245
Giles and the Birds

Giles loved watching the birds that came into his garden. There were blackbirds, starlings, jays and bluetits. But of all the birds that came there, Giles loved the cheeky house sparrows best of all.

Each day, Giles sprinkled breadcrumbs, nuts and bacon rind on to the bird-table. He put out fresh water, too, of course.

In the spring, he noticed that a pair of sparrows were building a nest just under the roof of his house. They were very busy flying to and fro with twigs, straw and leaves. Giles found some long grasses for them, too, and put them on to the bird-table. One sparrow swooped down and took two long grasses in its beak and flew back with them to the nest.

Giles laughed. 'First I help to feed the birds, then I help them to build a nest. I wonder,' he mused, 'when the little fledglings are born, if I could help them to fly . . . ?'

 **247**

Nicholas the Dreamer

'I like autumn best,' sighed Nicholas the dreamer. 'That's when I have the most fun.

'The woods are then in their best colours, the birches and the oaks go russet and brown and yellow in colour.

'When I grow up,' he thought, 'I'm going to be a painter and will paint all these wonderful colours of the autumn.'

Nicholas picked some shining chestnuts from where they had fallen on to the dry moss, and collected some mushrooms and golden nuts.

Underneath the great oak and chestnut trees he could see the squirrels' tracks which led to their winter stores of nuts. They knew where to find them but they didn't always find enough of them to see them through the winter.

The squirrels were friends he'd known for a long time, and when their stores ran short, Nicholas would feed them to keep them alive.

'Autumn is my favourite time of year,' said Nicholas.

 **248**

The Bugle

A squirrel was collecting nuts in the garden when he found a bugle.

'Now, whatever is that for?' he mused. He picked up one end and held it to his nose. It didn't smell of anything.

Then he tried to take a bite out of the side of it, but it was much too hard.

'Well, I can't smell it or eat it,' said the squirrel. 'Whatever is it for?'

The tomcat from the next-door garden joined him. 'It's a new mousetrap,' he boasted. 'The mice run in at the wide end,' he explained, 'and find they can't get out at the narrow end. Then I come and get them!' he finished with a grin. He fished his paw inside the bugle and pulled it out again. There were no mice.

'Hm,' said the squirrel, who hadn't believed a word the cat had been saying. 'So, we can't eat it or smell it and it can't catch mice. Whatever is it for?'

Just then, a little boy ran into the garden and picked up the bugle. He blew it and out came a very strange noise.

'So *that's* what it's for!' said the squirrel.

Daddy to the Rescue!

Martin and Oliver were out walking in the woods.

'Let's go and look for some snails,' said Martin.

The two children stopped where two forest tracks crossed each other.

'Which way do we go?' asked Oliver.

'That way!' said Martin.

'No, it's that way – I recognise the trees,' said Oliver.

'No, it's that way – I remember those mushrooms!' replied Martin.

'Look, we'll each go our own way,' said Oliver.

'Yes, but what if I meet the big wolf in the woods? Who'll protect me from him?' asked Martin.

'I'll protect you,' said Oliver, 'you'll see – come this way with me!'

'I think we're lost,' said Martin.

'Of course we aren't,' said Oliver.

'Well, we can't walk about all night in the woods!' cried Martin.

It grew dark and the woods became blue and violet and full of shadows. The animals all went down into their holes.

Martin got frightened.

'Give me your hand,' said Oliver.

'Shh! What's that noise?' asked Martin.

'Hey there? Where are you both?' cried a voice.

'Daddy! Here we are!' shouted Oliver.

Martin and Oliver had had quite an adventure, but they were very pleased that Daddy had arrived to take them home!

 **250**

The Little Leaf

Right on the top of a great oak tree a little leaf was complaining to itself.

'What a sad leaf am I, attached to this tree by a thin stalk. How I'd love to fly away, just like a skylark, up into the sky so that I could see all the world below. I could even dive down and take a closer look at that lovely lake below me, at the foot of this silly tree that won't let me go!'

Day after day, the pretty little leaf sobbed and lamented its fate. It didn't even thank the sun for warming it or the breeze for cooling it.

Then, one day, the breeze grew colder and stronger and the first acorns began falling to the ground. The little leaf was torn from its branch and flew away through the air, far from its familiar oak tree.

It flew across the surface of the lake, now lashed with icy rain, and was whipped by the cold wind against a hedge, where it shivered in the bare branches.

Suddenly, the great adventure of flying round the world was over.

Then, the leaf heard a child's voice, 'Look, Mummy, what a pretty leaf! It's the first one of the autumn. Let's take it home to decorate the classroom.'

On Monday, the leaf was pinned up on the white classroom wall.

'Isn't it lovely!' exclaimed the children.

 **251**

Five Little Pigs

This little pig went to market,
This little pig stayed at home,
This little pig had roast beef,
This little pig had none,
And this little pig cried, 'Wee-wee-
*   wee-wee-wee,*
I can't find my way home.'

Rufus Goes on Holiday

Old Farmer Matthew was a happy man. He had the best little donkey in the village. His name was Rufus.

'Hup! Whoa!' cried Farmer Matthew.

When Rufus came home to his stable that evening, he found it was really very dark and very narrow.

The next morning, Rufus had gone.

'Where has he gone?' asked the rabbits.

'Gone on holiday,' said the hare.

Rufus was very happy by the seaside. He went looking for mussels, and cockles and crabs.

One morning, a few days later, Farmer Matthew found Rufus asleep in his stable again. He stroked the little donkey and said, 'Well! There you are! I'm very glad to see you back.'

Rufus was rather expecting blows and kicks, but instead he was patted – and it was the first time his master had done that.

'Yes, thank you, Farmer. I've had a lovely holiday.'

253

First Day at School

Mark, was Mrs Brown's younger son and it was his first day at school. He was a little frightened at leaving the familiar surroundings of home for a new world.

His Mother promised him a new toy and said she would take him to see a puppet show after school, but nothing would persuade him to go.

But of course he had to go to school if he wanted to be a wise man and learn to read lots of stories. His Mother said she would take him to the school herself.

When they got to the door of the school, there was a little boy crying outside. His name was Alan, and he was hanging on to his Mother's skirt. He didn't want to go to school either!

So Mark had an idea. 'What's the matter? Why are you crying? Don't you want to go to school? Come on – let's go in together!'

254

Geese

It's raining, it's pouring,
And we've no place to hide,
While you're asleep and
snoring
We huddle, wet, outside.

But we don't really mind,
you know,
For us it's nothing new.
We've got our feathers and
webbed-feet –
We're better off than you!

Picking Mushrooms

Come along now everyone,
Picking mushrooms can be fun!
Follow us and you will find
Lots of them. Leave none behind!

And if it should rain
None of us will cry.
We'll pick a giant mushroom,
And it will keep us dry.

255

A Little Cloud

The flowers in the field were very thirsty under the hot sun.

Beryl watered them with her garden can, but it wasn't enough for them.

Up in the sky, a little blue cloud came along.

'Perhaps it's got some rain it can drop?' said Peepcheep, the sparrow.

The sparrow flew right up to the little cloud and told it that the flowers were all very thirsty.

The little cloud graciously tipped some of its rain down on to the flowers.

They straightened up again, their colours came back again and they felt quite well again.

'Thank you, little cloud. Thank you, little sparrow!' they cried.

The little cloud went on its way to drop a little of its precious rain on some other thirsty flowers elsewhere.

Then, in a trice, she found herself dancing on the sea – gliding over the sparkling waves as light as a fairy.

Sally was wondering how far out to sea the shoes would take her, when she felt herself lifted into space and there she was, twirling round the moon!

She went all the way round once, then bump! Sally landed back in her room.

'Tea is ready,' called Aunt Emily.

'I hope I'm not too late,' said Sally.

'Of course not,' said Aunt Emily and winked. 'I saw to *that*!'

 **258**

The Dream Pony

I have a pony called Nothing-at-all,
I know it's the strangest of names.
He comes in the evening, whenever I call,
And we play the most marvellous games.

I ride him bareback – no saddle for me,
No bridle to harness his head.
We ride over mountains and jump over
*   seas,*
At dreamtime, when I'm in my bed!

257

The Dancing Shoes

Aunt Emily had given Sally a pair of dancing shoes. Since Aunt Emily was a witch, Sally thought they might be special.

Tucked inside one of the shoes was a birthday card which read:

Dance on the treetops,
Dance on the sea;
Round the moon and back again
In time for tea.

Happy Birthday. Love Emily.

Sally stepped into her dancing dress. Then she put on the shoes. No sooner had she tied the ribbons, when the shoes carried her to the top of the trees in her garden!

259

Piglet and the Farmer

'Come along, piglet,' said the farmer, 'we're off to the forest to look for truffles!'

Underneath an oak tree the farmer told the piglet to look for truffles.

The piglet got to work digging them up and whenever he found one, the farmer took it from him and put it in his basket.

Piglet wasn't very pleased at not getting any himself and when he'd dug up the tenth truffle, he ran away.

The mole, the fox and the owl asked him why he wasn't digging up truffles any more.

Piglet said that he had never been given any truffles for himself – not even one!

The animals of the forest thought their little friend was quite right to run away.

They all went to see the farmer and told him that piglet should be rewarded for his hard work.

'All right,' said the farmer. 'I'll give piglet three truffles and a special supper tonight.'

260

The Little Walnut

A little walnut was all alone on a walnut tree. It could see for miles over fields and woods. It was very happy.

Then the wind began to blow. It blew so hard that the little nut fell off the tree and it began to roll along very fast in the wind.

Mary was out in the woods looking for flowers and she saw the little nut. She picked it up, but it slipped from her grasp and began to roll along very fast again.

Mary ran after it, through the woods where the mushrooms grew.

Then she reached the land where the walnut trees grow and there was great rejoicing there – the Prince of Walnuts was getting married.

Mary danced with the little walnut trees, with the rabbits and the hares.

She was given some walnut wine to drink and then they all had a walnut cake.

She went home after saying goodbye to the little walnut, who was so pleased to be in walnut land again.

Diddy the Duck and the Hunter

Diddy the duck and her ducklings were swimming in the lake.

Frederick, the hunter, was hiding in the bushes and he had decided to shoot Diddy for his dinner.

Growly, the old farm dog, followed his master, but he didn't really like him very much.

'You'd better be careful,' he said to the brown hare, 'Frederick is going hunting today!'

The hare dashed off to warn all the other animals.

Frederick went on watching the duck and Growly understood that his master was after Diddy. 'He's going to shoot her for his dinner,' thought Growly. 'I'll have to warn her to go away!' So he barked loudly.

Frederick was angry with his dog for making such a noise.

But Diddy the duck got away and took her ducklings to a safer spot.

'I'll get that duck!' Frederick said. He put his shotgun down and walked towards the lake. But Growly picked up the gun and hid it in the bushes!

Diddy the duck and her ducklings and Growly all had a good laugh.

Now Frederick will have to find some other sport.

Father Whitebeard

Pauline went for a walk in the woods with her doll Poppy.

She felt tired after a while and slept against a tree trunk.

She was awakened by someone laughing and saying, 'Hey! little girl. Wake up!'

It was old Father Whitebeard.

He was wearing old clothes and his shoes weren't very clean. He had a long, white beard and sharp blue eyes that twinkled when he laughed.

'Are you lost in the wood, girl?' he asked.

Pauline wasn't sure what to reply.

'Here, come with me, and I'll show you how to get back to the road,' he said. 'I see your doll has broken an arm – I'll fix it for you!'

They walked along together to the old man's house.

Pauline didn't really want to go inside – suppose he was an old wizard?

'Sit down there, by the fire, and I'll glue the doll's arm on properly. You can help yourself to a piece of bread and some honey from my bees,' he said.

Pauline found the honey very good.

Then it was time to go.

'Thank you, Father Whitebeard. I'll come and see you another day soon,' said Pauline.

263

Nikki the Squirrel

It was the day of the Squirrels' Oak Tree Race and Nikki had entered for it.

Each competitor had to race holding an acorn, which you may think sounds easy but, when I tell you that they had to run up one oak tree and down another, perhaps you will change your mind.

'Ready, steady,' called Felix Fox from the starting line.

Nikki dropped his acorn.

Felix began again. 'Ready, steady, go!'

The squirrels were off.

Nikki scrambled up the first oak tree, closely followed by a mean-looking fellow called Sam. Together they leaped across to the second oak tree. Nikki was running, head first down the trunk, when Sam deliberately tripped him over!

Poor Nikki fell head over tail onto the ground. Sam, who had followed him down the other side, grabbed at a bushy tail that was just disappearing round the tree trunk. Unfortunately for Sam, Nikki wasn't on the other end of it but Mr Felix Fox was! He had come to see what all the trouble was about.

Sam was sent home in disgrace, while Nikki ran on to win the race and a store of best hazelnuts. Well done, Nikki!

264

The Monkey

'What a smart monkey Simon is!' exclaimed Julia.

Peter burst out laughing and said, 'Smart? He's just a silly monkey!'

Julia challenged Peter to climb the tree in the garden faster than Simon.

'Done!' said Peter. 'He can't do it as fast as I can, you'll see!'

Of course, the monkey was an expert at climbing trees and he got to the top long before Peter.

Peter had to admit defeat and he also had to admit that Simon was a very smart monkey!

Paul and the Wounded Rabbit

Autumn had arrived. It was a beautiful Sunday afternoon and although Paul was feeling rather lazy, he felt he ought to go for a walk.

'Come on, Daddy,' he said. 'Let's go to the woods.'

Paul's Father was dozing in front of the fire, but he agreed to go.

The sun was shining on the russet, gold and brown leaves, and the air was crisp. Paul had a marvellous time kicking the leaves and crunching them under his feet.

All too soon it was time to go back home. They were almost there when suddenly they heard a whimper and found a terrified rabbit with its paw caught in a cruel, steel trap.

Paul and his Father gently released the rabbit and carried it home. Paul's Mother washed the rabbit's wound and dressed it and they cared for it for some while.

When the rabbit seemed quite well again, Paul took it back to the woods and watched it scamper happily away.

266

The Letter Box

'Look!' said the village children. 'The old lady has gone away – let's give her a surprise present.'

She had left her letter box wide open and the children put some flowers in it for her.

But the old lady didn't come back that day, nor the next.

Had she gone to visit her grandchildren?

The flowers died and became very dry and one day, a skylark made a nest in the nice, dry stalks and leaves.

When the old lady returned and opened the gate of her garden, she heard the skylarks singing from her letter box.

'Well!' exclaimed the old lady. 'Isn't that nice of the skylarks to choose my letter box to make their nest in!'

Mitzy Loses Her Kittens

'Miaou! Miaou!' mewed Mitzy the cat, as she walked through the forest all alone. 'They've given all my little kittens away! I'm so unhappy!'

And she sobbed as she walked along.

Up in the oak tree, a family of squirrels heard her and wondered what they could do to help. Mrs Squirrel had lots and lots of little squirrels to care for, so she thought it would be a good idea to ask Mitzy to look after three of her little squirrels.

She hurried down the tree and told the cat what she had decided.

Mitzy was very happy. She climbed up into the oak tree to meet her little foster children. They were russet-coloured, with beautiful long tails.

'We'll all live in the old oak tree,' said Mrs Squirrel.

It was quite a new sort of life for Mitzy the cat and very pleasant to have three little animals to look after. They all followed her when she went walking in the woods. But they didn't like mice or rats, they preferred nuts.

That didn't matter so long as everyone was happy together.

Mitzy purred with pleasure. She would never return to her old home. She preferred to stay with the animals of the forest, her new friends.

Back to School

The holidays were over and Max was on his way to school. He had a new school satchel under his arm, a new blue jacket and a magnificent pencil case as well.

In the school playground he saw a poor little boy called David, who had nothing new for the new term and was looking rather sad.

'Hallo, David!' said Max. 'Did you spend your holidays by the sea?'

'No, we stayed in the city,' answered David.

Max thought of the wonderful holiday he'd had under blue skies, where such interesting things were always happening – processions and fairs and where they enjoyed sandy beaches and hot sun.

He looked at David, who was not a bit suntanned but rather pale, and Max felt very sorry for him.

'Here,' he said suddenly, 'I've brought a present back from holiday for you . . .'

And Max gave David the pencil case he was so proud of.

The Wild Horse

The wild horse had run so fast and so far that he had to stop to get his breath back. He had only the wind and the clouds for company.

He sniffed the air – he could smell the smoke of a camp fire on the evening wind.

The wild horse trotted down hill towards a column of blue smoke by the stream.

'You must be very thirsty, wild horse,' said Paul, stroking the horse's beautiful brown mane.

The wild horse replied, 'I was thirsty for water – and for friendship, too!'

'Then stay with me, wild horse,' said Paul. 'I'll build you a shelter from the tall reeds.'

The wild horse rested his head a moment on Paul's shoulder and said, 'Yes, I'll stay a while. We'll go for a long gallop across the plains under the starry skies and we'll wait till the sun rises before going to sleep.'

'I'd like that very much,' said Paul.

271

The Big Race

Muffin was a racehorse. He shared a warm stable with a donkey called Hector and they were the best of friends.

'Do you know,' said Muffin sadly, 'I have never won a race.'

'Cheer up,' said Hector, 'I have never *run* in one before!' Then he poked his head over the stable door and chewed some thistles that were growing outside. 'My Mother once told me, "*Eat thistles in May, and lucky you'll stay.*" Try some,' he said to Muffin.

'It happens to be June,' said Muffin.

'Well, have some anyway,' said Hector.

The next day, Muffin's owner took him to the racecourse in a horse-box. It was the day of the Big Race and there were lots of other horses there.

Soon it was time for the race to begin and they were off! Muffin felt himself flying along, faster than ever and, before he knew what was happening, he was galloping first past the winning post.

'I told you those thistles were lucky,' said Hector, when Muffin returned that evening. 'My Mother is always right!'

270

The Antelope

Still as a statue,
Head held up high,
The Antelope watches the world go by.

Swift as an arrow,
Light as a bird,
The Antelope runs and follows the herd.

Where shall I find him?
Where does he roam?
On Africa's grasslands – that is his home.

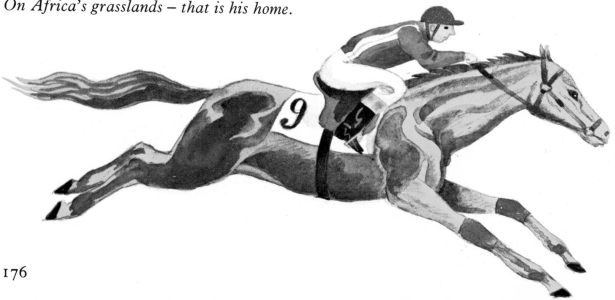

272

A Bunch of Grapes

One day, a very strange thing happened to a bunch of grapes. It grew so big that each grape became as big as a balloon!

Lots of birds came along and lived in these huge grapes, birds of all sorts of colours and sizes. Then, along came lizards and butterflies and fieldmice.

It was a very strange residence because instead of drying up, the grapes got stronger every day until they were able to resist the frosts of winter, the snow and the rain and the wind!

The animals who lived there made the grapes so warm and inviting that all sorts of other animals came along to live there as well – there were birds from the Arctic, and squirrels and starving fieldmice and lots more.

Then, all round this huge bunch of grapes there grew a strong, thick hedge that protected all the animals living there, and they were all very happy.

The news of this big, comfortable home spread so quickly that soon every grape on the bunch had an occupant. Would you believe it if I told you that there were one hundred animals living in that remarkable bunch of grapes!

273

The Old Chair

'I *hate* housework!' sulked Susan in a temper one day. She slapped the old chair with her duster and a cloud of dust flew up and made her cough.

'Serve you right!' said the chair.

Susan could not believe her ears.

'As a matter of fact,' said the chair, 'I do not like you sitting on me, but I have never refused you my seat. You kick my legs with your shoes, you never sit still and now you cannot even dust me without causing me pain!'

'Oh dear,' cried Susan. 'Poor, kind old chair, I am so sorry. Please forgive me.' Then she gently dusted the chair all over, until there wasn't a speck of dust to be seen on it.

The chair shone with pride.

Now Susan dusts the old chair very carefully every day, and when she sits down . . . she keeps perfectly still!

274

The Little Koala Bear

Koala Bear was sitting in his eucalyptus tree, feeling very full after lunch.

At the foot of the tree, Rabbit was running on the spot.

'What are you doing?' asked Koala Bear.

'Keeping fit,' panted Rabbit. 'Try it.'

Koala Bear climbed down with some difficulty. His tummy *was* very fat.

'Bend over and touch your toes,' said Rabbit, bending up and down a few times.

Koala Bear couldn't reach his knees!

'Try this then,' said Rabbit, kicking his back legs up to touch his front paws.

It was no good. Koala Bear struggled with his left leg and toppled over.

'It seems to me,' he laughed, 'one has to *be* fit to *keep* fit! I'll try again tomorrow,' he promised, and climbed home to bed!

Sarah Picks Mushrooms

Sarah hung a little basket on her arm and went off to the woods to pick mushrooms. Her dog, Ned, dashed on ahead sniffing at everything, looking for traces of rabbits. Under their feet, all the twigs and dry leaves crackled and crunched.

'Look! There's a funny looking mushroom – it's got a red hat and little green spots on it. But leave that one alone – it's poisonous! And there's another, all yellow – but that's no good either, that's poisonous, too.'

Sarah walked on further into the woods and looked under some bushes.

'Perhaps there'll be some good ones here,' she thought. 'Yes, there are some real mushrooms!' and she picked them and put them in her basket.

Ned barked and ran about joyfully. Then, he saw Sarah's Daddy coming along and rushed off to meet him. He had a basket too and it was full of juicy mushrooms that he'd collected. They did smell good.

'Mummy will be pleased,' said Sarah to her Daddy.

When they got home, Sarah helped her Mummy to peel the mushrooms. She was going to make a delicious mushroom pie.

Ned scampered about and barked. He wanted a piece of the pie too!

276

A Fine Residence

Up on a hill, there stood an old, abandoned castle, almost in ruins.

The great stag decided to live in it.

'Yes, it would be fine for the winters,' said the delighted fieldmouse.

The owls, the warblers and the finches all said the same.

So everybody moved in. The spiders threaded needles, the weaver birds worked very hard and soon everywhere looked very cosy.

Then winter came and it was surprised to find that its coldest wind couldn't penetrate the roof or the walls, so it called the snow to help it.

The snow fell, but it just melted on the roof.

The winter went back to the north, the spring came, making everything new and green again, and the animals were very proud of their new home.

277

Melanie the Vain Little Pig

Ever since the day she had modelled for a young painter, Melanie, a chubby young pig, had been very vain. She was fond of saying to her brothers and sisters, 'You'll see my portrait in an exhibition one day!'

And she said it so many times, they began to get rather bored with her.

Every evening she curled her little pink tail, using a very large curler, and never went to sleep before she'd polished her hooves and cleaned her face properly.

One day, when visiting the market, she saw her portrait inside a pork butcher's shop, and underneath it said, 'Tasty pork sold here'.

Melanie fled, and ever since then she has been much nicer!

Margaret and the Little Kid

'Margaret looks a little run down,' said her Mother one day. 'Let's send her to Uncle Henry's farm for a holiday.'

Margaret was delighted.

She ran after the little goats, looked for tadpoles in the ponds, and climbed on to the back of the little donkey in the field.

'Here's a present for you,' said Uncle Henry one day. 'This baby goat got separated from his Mother.'

The little kid soon grew quite tame.

But as time went on, the little kid would wander farther and farther away from the farm.

'What are you looking for, little kid?' Margaret asked him. But he never answered.

At the edge of the forest, the mother goat was watching and waiting.

'Ah, there you are, my little kid!' she said. 'At last I've found you!'

279

The Peanuts

'Frances, eat your meat! Frances, drink your soup! Frances, eat your bread!'

That's what Frances's Mother was always saying to her, and Frances didn't take much notice.

Frances was a pretty red-haired girl who much preferred peanuts, biscuits and sweets. 'Why should I eat meat and bread and soup when I don't want to?' she asked herself.

Well, as you see, Frances was a rather choosy little girl. But you'll see how she was punished for this rather unfortunate attitude.

One morning, refusing her breakfast as usual, Frances was very hungry at ten o'clock. Her Mother had gone shopping so Frances searched the kitchen for something to eat that she really liked.

She opened the pantry door and there was a huge packet of peanuts. What luck! Greedy Frances soon finished most of the packet.

At lunch, of course she wasn't hungry at all. Mother scolded her. That afternoon, Frances went as pale as a lily.

Her Mother looked worried, took her temperature and sent for the doctor.

He came and examined her.

'Nothing to worry about – just a touch of indigestion,' he said cheerfully.

A few days later, Frances felt much better and, thoroughly ashamed of herself, confessed to her Mother what she'd done and promised never to eat between meals again.

Lucy Locket

Lucy Locket lost her pocket
Kitty Fisher found it.
There was not a penny in it,
But a ribbon round it.

The Little Postman

'I'm the postman,' declared Christopher, setting a peaked cap on top of his fair hair. Then he filled a satchel with dead leaves which he collected in the forest, and set off on his rounds.

'This one's for you, Mr Owl . . .'

'Tu-whit, tu-whoo!' exclaimed Mr Owl as he read the maple leaf. 'I'm delighted.'

'Here's one for you Mrs Weasel,' said Christopher as he handed her a yellowing oak leaf.

'Important news!' announced Mrs Weasel. 'I'm invited to my cousin Mole's wedding.'

Christopher pedalled on along the forest path delivering post to the birds, the squirrels and the beavers.

'I hope,' he said at the end of his rounds, 'that you've all had good news.'

'Very good,' chorused the woodland animals.

They all stood around a pile of dead leaves which Christopher's Father had set alight, and chatted eagerly about their news.

Christopher felt very proud. He thought that he would be a postman when he grew up, because he liked making people happy.

Tom and the Bird

Tom was on his way to school. He was feeling happy.

'Tweet, tweet.' A baby bird flew on to the grass.

Tom caught him gently, saying, 'Come on, little bird, come with me.'

'Hurry up, Tom,' called the teacher.

'I've caught a little bird.'

The children whispered, 'It's only a baby.'

They soon made it a nest. They found some dead leaves, three soft feathers and a pretty green ribbon. The sparrow had plenty of seed and breadcrumbs, and lots of affection.

One fine morning, he chirped brightly and then off he flew through the open window.

A Bold Explorer

John was always top of the class in geography. He was the best at composition, too. Peter asked him, 'How come you're so good at those subjects?'

'Because of my brother, Jim. He's terrific!'

Jim was a student and wanted to find out all about the world. Every year he went on a trip to a foreign country, often a long, long way from home. Once he went to Africa to help some of the people cultivate their land; another time he went to India; and later to Japan. He described every exciting detail of his adventures and had photos to show people too.

So, that's why John, who never dreamt about anything else but becoming a bold explorer, was always top in geography. And when John had to write a composition he found that easy too. He wrote stories about his brother's exciting adventures.

Mother Sweet-Herb

Mother Sweet-Herb lived alone in a cottage in the middle of a wood.

First thing every morning, when the dew was fresh, she gathered herbs for medicines, as well as flowers and seeds.

'Tap! Tap! Tap!' came a knock at the door.

'Come in,' answered Mother Sweet-Herb. 'Oh, it's you, Red Hare. What can I do for you?'

'Little Fox has a sore throat.'

'Here, take him this herb tea and a special preparation to put on his neck.'

'Oh, thank you, Mother Sweet-Herb.'

All the animals in the wood loved her.

One stormy night, there was a terrible wind which blew the roof off the cottage.

The magpie and the jay both sang out as loudly as they could, 'Come quickly to Mother Sweet-Herb's.'

All the animals rushed to the cottage. Mr Bear sawed some planks and Mr Boar planed them, then Mr Fox hammered in the nails, and Mrs Deer gathered dry straw. That evening, a delighted Mother Sweet-Herb slept in a cottage that was almost brand-new, thanks to the rabbits and the hares and all the animals in the wood.

Greedy Waddle-Duck

Waddle-Duck was so greedy that terrible things happened to him sometimes.

One morning, when he had eaten a large dish of mash, Waddle-Duck went and gobbled up the chickens' breakfast. Then he dabbled in the mud looking for worms. And he was still not satisfied!

He was looking for something else to eat, when suddenly he spied a fat slug slipping into an old jam tin.

Quickly, he poked his head into the narrow tin and caught the slug. What a feast! But oh, woe – his head was stuck. He shook it about and struggled to get free, but in vain.

The chickens were panic-stricken and fled. Only Bob, the old dog, took pity on him and set him free; but he teased him too. 'Oh, you did look funny,' said Bob. 'What a story this will make!'

285

Fancy Dress

Everyone in the little village made fun of Marmaduke. They thought his name was so funny! And not only that – he was also as round as a ball, and because of his rosy cheeks, everyone called him 'apple'.

One day, there was a fancy dress party in the village. The children could wear whatever they liked, and there was going to be a prize for the best costume.

Jackie came dressed very cleverly as a sunflower. Frank was wearing a lion costume and Julian was disguised as a rabbit.

When Marmaduke walked in, a ripple of laughter ran right through the crowd at the party. Marmaduke had come as an apple! His costume was a great success and he was the person who won first prize!

The Old Apple Tree

Standing in a field were some pretty apple trees with red and gold apples growing on them.

One of the trees was old and twisted. He was going to die and he felt very sad because the birds did not visit him anymore.

One morning, a robin settled in the apple tree. He was tired. He ate an apple and told the tree how delicious it was.

The apple tree wept with joy and his tears made a golden covering for his trunk. Fresh sap began flowing inside him and his strength returned. The apples grew big and bright red.

The robin was delighted and sang at the top of his voice. He made his home in the apple tree and his family came to join him.

The old apple tree had never been so happy in his life! Apples were growing on his branches again and the robin was his friend.

288

Fly Away Little Bird

Autumn had come. Already the trees had turned red and there were dry leaves all over the ground.

To earn some money, Phil was raking up leaves in Mrs Sage's garden next door. She was a wise old lady.

He suddenly came across a poor, cold little bird with a damaged wing in a corner of the garden. Phil was afraid that the bird would die, so he looked after it and fed it patiently. And the happiest thing for him was to see the little bird fly away to join its friends when it was better.

'You know, the best way to be in life is to be free!' said Mrs Sage watching it go.

289

Florence's Day Out

Florence lived on a water-lily leaf, at the edge of a lake.

One day, the little frog decided to go exploring in the wood. Hop . . . hop . . . hop . . . she went leaping on her way.

First she saw Fox and threw a spiky chestnut at him. He ran off in a very bad temper, so Florence hopped on to say hello to Owl.

Weasel had a sore foot and did not feel like playing, so Florence went boating with her friend Squirrel. But . . . SPLASH . . . silly Squirrel fell in the water! Fortunately, Beaver arrived just at the right time to fish him out.

Grey Rabbit was nibbling some tasty green shoots when Florence hopped up. She sat and ate some mosquitoes to keep him company.

Night fell quickly. 'Time to go home now,' called Owl.

Florence hopped on to a big lily leaf, and as she fell asleep she thought, 'What a lovely day I've had!'

290

The Roundabout Horse

Mr Mac was such a tired old man that he decided to have a rest. 'No more fairs for me,' he said. 'I'm going to sell the round-about.'

So he shut all the roundabout animals in a dusty shed, where they dreamt about the sunshine and the wind outside.

But Rusty, the little brown horse, said to the white cow, 'Cow, would you break this rope for me with your horns?'

The cow did what he asked and Rusty thanked him, then trotted away.

The little horse was beside himself with happiness and drank in the sun and the wind. He ran across fields, raced over hills after clouds, followed grassy tracks and frisked about in the forest on a carpet of gold and silk . . . How good it felt to be free!

But soon winter came with its cold and snow and Rusty was hungry. One day, he saw whispy blue smoke curling up through the trees. The woodcutter was lighting his fire. Rusty moved a little closer and the woodcutter saw him. He put a bunch of hay on the path.

Rusty nuzzled the dry, sweetly smelling hay.

He went even closer and said, 'I should like to be your friend.'

'Come on,' said the woodcutter. 'If I give you hay, you can tell me all about the fun of the roundabout.'

The Painter in the Woods

Johnny often went into the forest to paint.

One day he sat and painted an autumn scene, with its yellow and red trees.

The beaver came up and admired it.

'That is your best painting yet,' he said approvingly.

Then Johnny painted some leaves. He made them red and brown. And, after that, he added a pile of burning leaves. What a pretty picture it was now! The flames were all different colours – yellow, blue, red and even green.

'That's wonderful!' exclaimed the squirrels.

Johnny went home and hung his new painting in the picture gallery.

As always, the animals of the wood came and admired the artist's work. The deer was full of praise and congratulated him warmly.

Johnny was very proud. His parents thought he might be famous in a few years' time.

293

The Honey Bear

Barnaby lived in a circus. He was a large brown bear and he loved honey, lots and lots of it!

His trainer gave him a big pot every morning, but one day he ran out – there was no more honey for Barnaby, and he absolutely refused to work.

Barnaby's friend, a little girl, brought him some molasses and sugar and even some nice jam, but none of them would do!

Now, Edward the elephant knew of a tree where there was a beehive full of wild honey. Barnaby followed him there and chased away the angry bees. What a feast he had! Now he could go back to the circus and practise all his tricks.

Barnaby's trainer was delighted to see him back at work. That night Barnaby gave the best performance of his life, and his trainer made sure that he never ran out of honey again!

292

The Birthday Present

It was Mary's eighth birthday and her best friends decided to give her a special present.

Early that morning, the three little girls went shopping and loaded up their baskets until they could carry no more.

As soon as they got home, they set to work mixing and stirring, and by lunchtime they had finished making the special birthday present.

When it was time to go to Mary's party, the three girls carried the present carefully around to her house.

'Surprise! Happy birthday!' they called when she opened the door.

'Why, it's a beautiful, big chocolate cake!' exclaimed Mary, clapping her hands with excitement. 'What a lovely party we shall have!'

294

A Safe Hiding-Place

295

Off to School

As autumn drew near, Mother Squirrel taught her children how to gather walnuts and ripe hazelnuts so that they would have a food store for the winter.

'First, find some safe hiding-places in the hollows of old trees, then line them with moss and leaves,' said Mother Squirrel to her children.

Rupert, the smallest and the most lively of the squirrel children, was eager to get started. He scampered here and there carrying nice plump nuts to his secret hiding-places. But, silly Rupert forgot the way to his hollow tree and by the time evening came, he was in tears.

'What are you crying about?' asked the owl in a deep voice.

'Oh, dear,' sighed the little squirrel. 'All day I've been carrying my winter nuts to various stores. And now I've covered so much of the wood that I can't find my way back to them.'

'I've been watching you from the top of the oak tree,' said the owl. We will find your stores together. But from now on, you must put a special mark on the tree you have chosen so that you can find your way back to it.'

Up and away leaves flutter today,
And scurry away, and flurry away,
While all the children hurry away
Off to school today!
Up and around leaves whirl from the
*   ground,*
And rustle around and bustle around,
While all the children hustle around,
Off to school today!

296

Muffin and the Fox

There was once a little fox-cub who was lost in the woods. He felt very hungry as he lay amongst some ferns, trying to keep warm.

But it so happened that Bartholomew, the game-keeper, was walking through the ferns, and found the little fox. He tucked him under his waistcoat and carried him back to Diana, his little niece.

Diana raised the little fox on a bottle and called him Bernard. She was delighted with her new pet but Muffin, her dog, was a little jealous of the fox-cub.

Bernard grew into a handsome, well-behaved fox, and when his mistress took him for a walk he wore a collar and lead.

One day, Muffin became the proud mother of five dear little puppies, but she was left to raise them all by herself.

Bernard offered to help her and Muffin accepted. He played with the puppies and taught them lots of tricks. He took them into the woods and he showed them where all the other animals lived.

The five puppies were very happy and so was Muffin!

297

Rosie Pig

Rosie Pig promised her four little ones that she would take them on the train for an outing.

Waiting in the station were five big coaches and an enormous engine. The Little Pigs climbed awkwardly into the compartment. Sitting opposite them were two old ladies, who turned up their noses at the pigs.

Soon they were away! The two old ladies went to sleep and Rosie Pig did the same. But the Little Pigs could think of nothing more boring than sleeping. One of them caught sight of the old ladies' basket

– it was full of cakes! The four Little Pigs soon gobbled them all up.

Suddenly they heard the guard calling, 'End of the line, everyone off the train.'

One of the old ladies lifted up the basket and shrieked, 'It's empty!'

Rosie Pig knew exactly what had happened and hurried off the train with her four greedy little children.

299

Naughty Theodore

Mother Bear was very cross one morning because Theodore, her son, would not stop doing silly things.

Rushing to have his breakfast, he had tipped perfectly good, creamy milk all over himself. Mother Bear had had to wash him and then clean the kitchen.

When everything was back to normal, Theodore spotted a bee and decided to chase it. But chasing a bee inside is not easy and Theodore bumped into everything in his way. It was not long before the house was in a terrible mess.

Mother Bear felt quite helpless. What could she do with a naughty son like that!

Worn out, next morning she took Theodore to school. At last she could have some peace and quiet. The little bear looked very sad as he went into school, but Mother Bear stood firm. Besides, Theodore had to learn to read and write.

The day passed peacefully. Soon it was time for the children to come out of school. Mother Bear saw Theodore walking along the road with a happy group of children. Theodore had found some friends – now he would never be bored and perhaps not quite so naughty at home!

298

The Wolf and the Fox-Cub

'Oh I do wish I could find my Mother,' whimpered the little fox-cub. He had been parted from his Mother for hours.

As he pattered along the forest path, he spied an old hollow tree stump.

'At least I would be warm in there,' he thought. He climbed in and curled up snugly, and soon he was fast asleep.

As he slept, he felt something nudge his nose. He opened one eye sleepily and saw a wolf with her two babies.

'Come with me little fox. You look so unhappy all by yourself.'

The little fox-cub was delighted – he had a new Mother to look after him and some friendly little wolf-cubs to play with.

Ben and the Little Duck

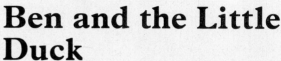

'Come on,' called Mandy to her dog. 'We're going for a walk in the forest.'

Ben barked happily and wagged his tail.

'Let's play hide-and-seek,' suggested Mandy because it was so cold in the snow.

She ran and hid behind a tree. Ben went looking for her, sniffing here and there.

'Bow-wow, found you,' he barked, running up to the tree.

'My turn now,' said Mandy. Ben scampered off and hid amongst some bushes.

Suddenly, he barked loudly and Mandy ran to his hiding-place. There, in the bushes, was a little duck with pretty brown and green feathers. He looked very tired and weak.

'We had better take him back to the farm as quickly as we can,' said Mandy.

When they got home, Mandy's Mummy looked after the little duck. Soon he felt better and he was very happy with the other ducks in the farmyard.

300

The Hedgehog

'Look what I've brought home!' said Andrew's Father, putting a big, dark prickly ball on the ground.

'What is it?' asked Andrew, a little frightened.

'Guess?...A hedgehog! He's not vicious but you can't touch him without pricking your fingers.'

After a few moments, the ball unwound and a little, pointed nose appeared.

'How funny he looks!' laughed Andrew. May I play with him?'

'No,' answered his Father, 'first he must get used to the house. In the spring we will make a home for him in the garden.'

'Perhaps he will eat some of the snails and slugs that nibble at your lettuces,' said Andrew.

'I do hope so,' said Andrew's Father.

302

The Last Rose

Jack Frost had not come to the flowers yet. In the middle of the garden there was a rosebush that was shaping her last rose.

'I'd be careful if I were you,' said the violet, peeping out from under her leaves. 'If Jack Frost comes, he will hurt your rose.'

'He won't come now,' replied the rose-bush. 'I have already seen the butterfly unfolding her wings.'

Early next morning, the bold rosebush unfurled her beautiful pink rose. Suddenly, an icy covering fell on her branches and froze the heart of her rose.

Wicked Jack Frost had arrived. But he took pity on the rosebush and decorated her with pretty silvery garlands. Then he sprinkled the heart of the rose with sparkling jewels of frost. And the whole garden was amazed at the beauty of the rosebush.

303

Broody Hen's Chickens

All the children in Jenny's class were very excited. She had just run in to the class-room to tell them that she had heard a tapping sound coming from Broody Hen's eggs. The hen had been sitting on her eggs for days.

The children all tip-toed up to Broody Hen's wire pen and gathered around.

'Tap . . . tap . . . tap,' came the sound of little beaks working inside the egg-shells. Suddenly, a hole appeared in one of the shells and out came a beak, followed by a pair of legs and a fluffy ball of yellow down.

The children whispered excitedly as they watched the chickens breaking out of their shells one by one. When all three little chickens had hatched, Broody Hen clucked proudly and nestled them gently under her soft, warm wings.

304

Sounds the Same

Here is another puzzle in which two words with very different meanings sound the same. Can you tell what they are from the clues?

You can mix some in a bowl to make delicious cakes or you can grow one of these in your garden.

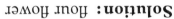

Solution: flour flower

305

Aunt Olivia

Aunt Olivia was a very quaint old lady and her nieces and nephews were always making fun of her. Sometimes she grumbled when the children were naughty, but she always had sweets in her pockets for them.

One day, she bought herself a new hat. It was a yellow hat decorated with artificial red cherries. When Aunt Olivia came visiting in her new hat, naughty Timothy thought of a trick to play on her. He and the other children looked in the kitchen and found some fresh cherries and grapes which his mother had just bought. Then he took the artificial cherries off Aunt Olivia's hat and replaced them with the real fruit! When it was time to go, Aunt Olivia put on her hat and said goodbye.

The children all wondered what Aunt Olivia would say the next day.

But, to their surprise, she arrived with a big smile on her face and said to them, 'What a clever trick you played on me! It did make me laugh, and the fruit was quite delicious. Now, if you would kindly take a needle and thread and sew the cherries on my hat, all will be well.'

Timothy's face fell, and he never played a trick on Aunt Olivia again.

306

Winter Fun

'Isn't it fun to go skating on the pond in winter,' said Eric to his friend Rob.

'I like skiing down the hills when the snow's thick enough,' replied Rob. Last year, my sister and I made a toboggan and it was so exciting to go whizzing down the hills with the wind whistling in our ears. Susie and Mark used to throw snowballs at our furry hats and Dick, the sheepdog, used to come with us and play in the snow.'

'Sometimes,' Rob went on, 'we let Dick have a ride on the toboggan with us. He used to love going fast down the hills. And when we got home, we would sit in front of the fire and dry out, and Mum would make us lovely big cups of hot chocolate.'

'I hope winter will be as much fun this year,' said Eric.

'Of course it will be,' said Rob. 'Come on let's go skating on the pond now and afterwards we will make a snowman. It's going to be better than last year.'

307

Silly Mr Fox

It was very cold and snowflakes were falling thick and fast in the forest. All the animals were curled up inside their homes, waiting for warmer days.

Mr Fox poked his nose out of his den – he was hungry! He looked all about with his sharp little eyes. Nothing moving!

He put one foot out slowly, then all four, and went trotting off, leaving paw marks in the fresh, smooth snow.

Suddenly, two long pointy ears popped up in the distance.

'Ah, what's that I see?' said Mr Fox excitedly. 'A tasty little bunny!' And he crept closer.

'Mmm, what a delicious lunch I shall have with such a fat, tender bunny!' and he licked his lips and closed his eyes dreamily at the thought of it.

The little bunny was too clever for Mr Fox and scampered off while he had his eyes closed.

'Oh, how silly I am,' moaned Mr Fox, and he went home feeling as hungry as he had when he set out.

Poor old Mr Fox!

308

Warm Clothes for the Snowman

The children were playing in the snow all day long, throwing snowballs and building a big snowman. Mark's Uncle George gave the snowman his old hat and one of his pipes, and he looked very handsome.

'It's time for bed, Mark,' said Mummy after dinner that night.

Mark hopped into bed but he could not sleep. He was thinking of the poor snowman, cold and all alone outside in the night.

Suddenly, he had an idea. He groped his way through the dark and found his Father's old overcoat and a woollen scarf. He carried them outside and dressed the snowman warmly, then hurried back to bed.

Feeling much happier about the snowman, he fell sound asleep.

310

Paul's Visitors

Paul was sick in bed with a cold. No-one had come to visit him and he was feeling bored. It was a cold day and he could hear all his friends playing outside. Why didn't they come in to see him? They must have forgotten all about him.

Then suddenly he heard a voice asking his Mother, 'Is Paul feeling better today?' In a moment, the door opened and in came the little girl and boy from next-door, carrying a storybook for him to read.

Paul was delighted and asked them both to stay and read some stories with him.

309

Frisky Goes Skiing

'No, no, no,' snorted Frisky the donkey. 'I refuse to spend all the winter shut up in my stable.'

'I agree,' declared Ned the horse. 'Why don't we go skiing on the mountain instead.'

'We had better wear our warm red hats and our furry boots,' suggested Clara the cow wisely.

Early the next morning, Frisky, Ned and Clara could be seen weaving their way down the ski runs through the powdery snow, riding back to the top on the chair-lifts and skiing down again at dizzy speeds . . .

'No more boring old stable for me!' shouted Frisky to his friends as they sailed down the snowy slopes together.

311

Oliver's Friends

'Look out Oliver, you'll fall.'

'Ooh, my leg . . . ooh!'

'Mummy . . . Daddy, come quickly. Oliver has hurt himself.'

Daddy carried Oliver inside and Mummy tucked him up in bed.

When the doctor came, he put Oliver's broken leg in plaster and said, 'Three weeks in bed for you, my boy.'

Outside in the garden, the birds were twittering in the hedge.

'He gave us some crumbs in winter,' said one.

'He put water out for us all through summer,' said his mate.

The two little birds flew into Oliver's bedroom carrying twigs, roots, a little piece of wool, some feathers, some moss and some horsehair. Then they made a nest in the corner.

'I shall lay my eggs here,' said the tit. 'Will that make you feel happy Oliver?'

'Oh, yes,' replied Oliver. 'Thank you little birds.'

312

The Ski Instructor

Pat, the little bear, was very happy. It was winter again and he had a nice thick fur coat to keep him warm. He would also be seeing his town friends again – they came to ski with Pat.

Pat was a champion skier. He raced down the slopes at unbelievable speeds and zig-zagged between the pine trees.

During the winter, Pat became a ski instructor. His pupils were not very talented. Often they would tumble to the foot of the slope, covered in a huge ball of snow.

One of them twisted his ankle and Pat had to take him down to the doctor in the village on a little sledge. It wasn't serious and a week later he was back on his skis again.

By the end of winter, all Pat's pupils were excellent skiers. They looked forward to the next winter when they would be able to follow Pat down the slopes.

313

Puzzle

Little Nanny Etticoat
In a white petticoat
And a red nose;
The longer she stands
The shorter she grows.

Solution: a candle

314

The Box of Chocolates

Daddy had given Nicola some money to spend. It was Mummy's birthday the next day, so Nicola bought her a beautiful box of chocolates and hid them in a drawer in her bedroom.

That night Nicola lay awake thinking about the chocolates. She wanted to see what they were like under their wrappers. So, she got out of bed and opened the box. They looked delicious.

'Mmm,' she said as she gobbled two of the chocolates, 'I'll have another of those.' She ate three chocolates with soft centres and then...another and another...until finally she had eaten all the chocolates in the box.

The next day, Nicola was sick.

'You had better go to bed,' said Mummy.

'Your daughter has eaten too many chocolates,' laughed Daddy as Nicola went sorrowfully off to bed. But he did not tell Nicola's Mummy that the chocolates were meant for her!

315

The Little Poet

'I don't like winter,' declared Frank's Mother with a shiver. 'It's so chilly and people catch awful colds and flu. Ooh, it's a wicked season!'

'Don't be silly!' said Frank's Father who was sitting comfortably in his armchair. 'It's lovely to be at home in front of the fire with the paper, a good pipe and a cup of coffee.'

But Frank felt differently about winter. He was waiting impatiently for the first snow and the snowmen he would make and the tobogganing . . . And he told his parents how he loved to see the countryside when it was covered in a thick, white blanket of snow!

'Why, we have a real poet in the family,' said his Mother kindly. 'You're quite right Frank, it's simply a matter of being able to see the good side of things!'

316

Little Grey Wolf

Little Grey Wolf ran through the wood looking for someone to play with.

He saw a squirrel gathering nuts at the foot of a tree. Little Grey Wolf chased him round and round until the squirrel ran up the tree in fright and disappeared amongst the branches.

Next, Little Grey Wolf found a group of rabbits playing. He ran to join them but they were frightened of him, too, and scampered away.

A strong wind blew through the trees and sent the leaves on the ground scurrying into the air. Little Grey Wolf thought that was fun. First he chased the leaves – then they chased him. What a game they had! Then the wind died down and it was time for Little Grey Wolf to go home.

317

The Shadow Game

The rain was pattering on the roof outside and the children had run out of games to play.

'What shall we do now?' said Jenny.

Andrew suddenly had an idea. They would play shadow games. He went first, and the shadows he made on the wall with his fingers became the characters in a little play.

The others sat on the floor and watched. 'What a good game for a rainy day!' they all agreed.

318

Dogs and Cats

'Dogs are man's best friends,' declared Robert, 'and my dog, Bimbo, is the most faithful and loving of all.'

Sonia was tired of hearing about Bimbo and thought that her wonderful cat, Whiskers, was not appreciated enough in the house. But, one day, something happened that made Whiskers a hero.

One evening, when all the family were sitting reading around the fire, Whiskers began to miaouw loudly beside Father's armchair. Father's pipe had fallen out of the ashtray and the woolly rug had begun to burn. It was Whiskers who had noticed the little flames. Everyone made a great fuss of him and Sonia felt very proud of her clever cat.

319

The Rabbit's New Home

One icy morning in winter, Don set off to collect some logs of wood that his Father had cut in the forest.

'Be quick now,' said Mummy. 'It's going to snow.'

Don hurried off and soon found the pile of logs in the snow. But what was this? Huddled in a corner of the pile was a baby rabbit. He was a long way from his burrow and very cold.

Don lifted him up gently and put him inside his coat. Then he picked up the logs and walked briskly home through the snow which was falling heavily now.

Don found a box for the rabbit, and kept him warm and fed him. The rabbit liked his new home so much that he stayed and lived in the garden.

320

Bright Red Boots

Helen was as happy as could be! Mummy had bought her some beautiful red boots with fur inside.

What fun it was to walk in the snow in her lovely new boots! They were so soft and warm that she wore them on long walks in the country and she never ever had cold feet.

321

The Dance of the Crayons

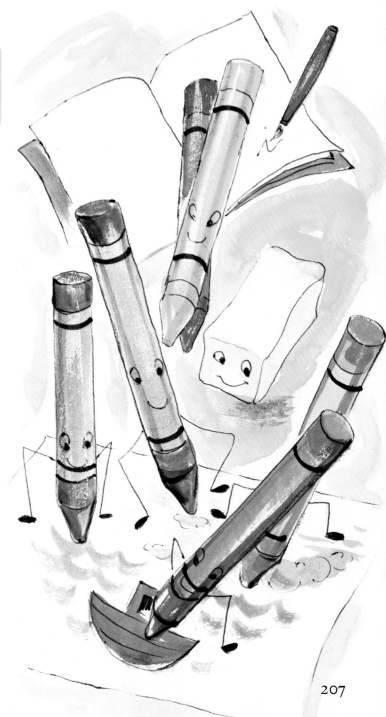

David was so tired one night that he went to bed without finishing his homework and left it lying on his desk.

He had a smart red pencil case which held twenty-four coloured crayons, a rubber and some pens. When David had gone to bed, they all decided to give him a special surprise and finish his homework for him. His essay was called 'My Holiday'.

The rubber bounded here and there, wiping away mistakes and dirty marks. The pen hopped about, crossing the 't's' and dotting the 'i's'. The crayons were busy with David's holiday drawing. The blue one coloured in the sky, while the pink one drew some delicate clouds. The turquoise crayon danced up and down, drawing little waves around the bright red boat. And to finish the picture, the yellow crayon drew a lovely big sun.

When they had finished, they all climbed into the pencil case and lay quite still.

What a marvellous surprise for David in the morning!

David's teacher collected his homework and when she had finished reading it she said, 'Your essay is so good there is a touch of magic about it!'

A Stormy Day

Redtail, the little squirrel, was coughing and sneezing. He had caught a cold from playing in the puddles. His Mummy said that he had to stay warm in bed. He could hear his friends chasing each other through the trees and he wanted to go and join in, but his Mummy was keeping a watchful eye on him. Poor little Redtail felt quite miserable.

Suddenly, the sky went black. Big drops of rain splashed down on the grass and thunder growled. Redtail's friends all hurried off home as the storm crashed through the forest. It was going to be a boring day for the little squirrels.

'I know,' said one, 'we could go and see Redtail.' So they all scampered across to Redtail's house and burst in the door crying, 'Hello Redtail, we've come to play with you!'

Redtail was so pleased to see them.

The little squirrel sat up in bed and they all played together for the rest of the day. As his friends left to go home, Redtail said, 'I'm sure to be feeling better to-morrow and we can play together in the trees.'

323

Marmalade and Meredith's Concert

Marmalade and Meredith were two little cats. They had promised their friends that they would sing for them, and the concert was tonight.

Aunt Thelma had made them some lovely clothes – for Marmalade, a pair of trousers with a big green belt and, for Meredith, a bright blue dress.

The two little cats waited nervously in the wings.

'I'm scared,' whispered Meredith.

'So am I,' replied Marmalade.

There were lots of their friends in the audience. With a deep breath, Marmalade and Meredith danced on to the stage and began to sing. The audience listened, wide-eyed.

'Don't they sing beautifully,' someone whispered.

After each song the audience clapped and tossed flowers on to the stage. Marmalade and Meredith were very pleased and asked their friends to join with them in one last song.

What a grand performance it was!

324

At Brill on the Hill

At Brill on the hill
The wind blows shrill,
The cook no meat can dress;
At Stow-on-the-Wold,
The wind blows cold,
I know no more than this.

326

Little Pussy

I love little pussy,
Her coat is so warm,
And if I don't hurt her
She'll do me no harm.
So I'll not pull her tail,
Nor drive her away,
But pussy and I
Very gently will play.

325

A Trip to the Zoo

One sunny day, Patrick and Prudence went with their Mummy to the zoo.

Both the children loved looking at pictures of animals in books, but it was much more exciting being close to them and talking to them and feeding them peanuts.

They thought the monkeys were the funniest, with their shrill little squeaks. Mother bear was so big and clumsy that she made them laugh, too. And they were thrilled when the elephant and the giraffe came out of their houses to say hello.

The penguins were great fun to watch and so were the sea-lions, especially at feeding time.

Patrick and Prudence did not have time to see all the animals, but they promised to go on another trip to the zoo very soon.

327

The Three Little Kittens

Mrs Brown had three little kittens. Two were grey and very naughty and one was ginger and very good. The grey kittens were called Tim and Tom and the ginger kitten was just called Kitty.

Tim was very fond of fishing from a boat. Poor Mrs Brown was always rescuing him. Tim would lean too far over the side of the boat to see if he had caught anything . . . and fall in! Tom preferred catching mice . . . in other people's gardens. Poor Mrs Brown was always rescuing *him* from angry neighbours' cats.

Kitty, however, was quite different. She preferred to play the violin! Now, whenever Tim and Tom are naughty, Mrs Brown makes them listen to Kitty practising her violin. The sound is so dreadful that Tim and Tom try hard to be good!

328

Toys in the Window

Snug and warm inside his little red coat and hat, Jonathan stood gazing at all the toys in the bright shop window.

And when he turned away to walk on down the street, it was just as if he were stepping out of fairyland – a world of fun and colour and magic.

329

The Magic Griffin

The Magic Griffin was asleep beneath the willow tree. He was a wonderful creature with the head and wings of an eagle and the body of a lion. Suddenly, he was woken by Martha, the wood-pigeon.

'Oh Magic Griffin, we're all so afraid! There's a hunt coming this way, and we don't know what to do.'

In the clearing, all the little animals clustered round the Magic Griffin.

The hunting party soon arrived with their dogs. Not a sound could be heard from the woodland animals. There were no birds singing and no animal scents for the dogs to follow. The dogs refused to go on, so the huntsmen called them back and left the woods.

All the birds started singing at once, in praise of the Magic Griffin.

330

Fairy Magic

Have you ever wondered how the woodland fairies decorate their Christmas tree?

On moonlight nights the fairies fly with cobweb sacks to gather the tiniest, brightest stars. And when the cobweb sacks are so full that not even a speck of stardust can be fitted in, the fairies slide back down to earth on moonbeams.

Then, on Christmas Eve, the fairies hang the tiny stars on the prettiest fir tree for all the woodland folk to see.

331

The Mushroom Without a Hat

One day there was a great hubbub in the field. Tiny, the dove, flew from tree to tree announcing that a little mushroom had been born without a hat.

'What are we going to do?' wondered the mushroom parents anxiously.

'Try my bell on him,' suggested the kindly bluebell. But, alas, it was too small.

Then the daisy placed a crown of daisy petals on the little mushroom's head, and everyone said how pretty he looked. But he took it off, saying indignantly, 'I'm not a flower!'

Soon it began to rain and the little mushroom was very unhappy. Tiny found one half of a nut-shell and put it on his head. It was too big and he looked like a soldier in it. Father mushroom collected some blades of grass and put them on his son's head.

'How handsome you look now!' exclaimed all the field-dwellers. And they gathered round him in a circle. But, a little sheep who was grazing there looked curiously at this strange thing with grass on its head and ate the grass greedily. So the little mushroom found himself without a hat again.

'It's all right,' said his Father. 'You will be the only mushroom in the field without a hat!'

'And that makes me very special, doesn't it?' said the little mushroom brightening up.

'It certainly does,' said his Father.

332

Cock-a-Doodle-Doo!

Every morning, just as the sun was about to come up over the hills, the rooster would cry out as loud as he could, 'Cock-a-doodle-doo!' Then he would stand looking proudly at the sun as it rose over the hills.

'I am the one who tells the sun to come up,' he declared grandly to the admiring hens.

But, one day, wicked little Vincent, the farmer's son, came well before dawn and shook the rooster, who was sound asleep in the hen-house.

'It's late Mr Rooster,' said Vincent, 'it's time you were waking up the sun.'

Still half-asleep, the rooster crowed and crowed . . . but the sky stayed black and the sun did not rise. Feeling very unhappy, the rooster went and hid in the darkest corner of the hen-house, while the hens gossiped and made fun of him.

333

A Quiet Evening

All the family were sitting together comfortably around a warm, crackling fire. Father was reading, Mother was sewing and Sam, the eldest of the children, was talking to his two sisters.

'Right now,' he was saying, 'I would like to be in the mountains, skiing and skating.'

'I would like to be in the big city,' sighed Leonie dreamily, 'then I could go to dances and the theatre . . .'

'I just want to stay here with all of you,' murmured little Bessie, climbing on to her Mother's knee.

'That's good,' said Mother, kissing her gently. 'I'm glad that one of you is content to stay at home.'

334

A Trip Round the World

'Rat-a-tat-tat! Rat-a-tat-tat!' Louisa went striding down the road, beating on her drum.

'Where are you going Louisa?' called a friend.

'I am going on a trip round the world!'

'Aren't you scared, going off all by yourself, so far from home?'

'I'm not afraid of anything,' replied Louisa proudly.

Suddenly, the dog from next-door appeared at the corner of the street and came towards Louisa, barking loudly. Louisa dropped her drum and ran as fast as she could back to her house. And that was the end of her trip round the world.

335

Ice on the Pond

Nicky and Virginia were walking quietly through the forest, the sound of their footsteps muffled by the snow.

'Oh!' cried Virginia. 'Look, the pond is frozen over.'

'So it is,' cried Nicky. 'We could go skating in our boots.'

They whipped around happily on the ice, slipping and sliding, laughing and shouting.

Suddenly, Virginia sped ahead and couldn't stop herself. A tree loomed up and . . . bang! Virginia was sprawled on the ground with a huge bump on her forehead.

Nicky picked up his sister and comforted her. 'It's nothing serious. Don't cry.' And he put a wet handkerchief on the bump. Virginia felt better then and they slowly made their way home. They would be more careful the next time they went sliding on the pond.

And they were.

336

The New Law

An owl was sitting in a wood when a hungry fox came by. The owl flew into a tree for fear the fox might eat him.

'Don't be afraid,' said the cunning fox. 'There is a new law in this wood that forbids animals to harm one another. Come down here and we will talk together.'

The owl knew better than to trust the fox. 'I can see better from up here,' he said. 'For instance, I can see a fine pack of hounds heading this way.'

The fox began to run away. 'Don't be afraid,' chuckled the owl. 'I thought you said that there was a new law – surely the hounds will not harm you now?'

'That may be so,' said the fox, 'but some animals haven't heard about it yet!'

Columbus Has an Adventure

Columbus had black, silky fur, a white nose, white paws and magnificent whiskers. He was a rather special cat because he was not only very affectionate, but also as agile as a panther. However, he did have one fault – he was very curious.

Now, this is what happened to curious Columbus . . .

It was winter, when nights were long and all sensible people and animals went to bed early in their warm houses, safe from the cold and snow. But, Columbus was not afraid of the cold or the wind and, being curious to explore the calm, quiet countryside, he went out one evening. No-one could stop him going.

So off he went, braving the icy wind, nosing about here and there, sniffing everywhere. Then, behind the neighbour's farmhouse, Columbus heard a strange noise. Very quietly, he crept closer, and what should he see but a handsome fox! He was sniffing, too, but more seriously. He was sneaking up on some little chickens for his dinner!

Suddenly, he caught sight of Columbus who realised too late what danger he was in. The fox was after him now, running so fast that poor Columbus was panting. But Columbus was too cunning for the fox, and he scrambled up a tree, leaving his enemy, disappointed, down below.

Early in the morning, Columbus stumbled home exhausted, vowing that he would stay inside in the warm, safe from any more adventures.

Columbus is still a very beautiful cat but he is not quite so curious now!

338

The Clown

The children were all sitting by the fire, huddling in a group around Grandfather, who was sitting in his armchair. They were all busy making plans for the future.

'When I grow up, I am going to be a general,' declared Hugh.

'I'm going to be a nurse,' said Angela in a quiet voice, 'and I will look after the soldiers.'

Then David spoke up. He was a little rascal and always up to tricks, and he said, 'I'm going to be a clown so that I can make people laugh and feel happy.'

'And I shall be very proud of you all,' said Grandfather.

339

The Man in the Wilderness

The man in the wilderness asked of me,
'How many strawberries grow in the sea?'
I answered him, as I thought good,
'As many as herrings grow in the wood.'

340

The Old Gardener

It was a cold winter in the forest.

The warbler called to the blue tit.

The blue tit called to the blackbird.

The blackbird whistled to the jay.

And the jay made an announcement to all the animals, saying, 'The old gardener who lives all alone in the forest is ill. Come quickly!'

The fox, the boar, the buck and the doe all ran through the forest to the old man's house. The poor gardener was shivering in his untidy bed.

The boar cut some logs and soon had a lovely warm fire blazing merrily.

The fox drew some water from the well.

The doe made a special preparation for colds and some herb tea, and the buck filled a hot-water bottle.

The old gardener lay back in his soft, warm bed and drank his tea, while the birds twittered around him.

'You'll be well again soon.'

'Thank you,' replied the gardener, 'I feel much better already.'

341

Unfriendly Polly

Polly, the pigeon, lived on a farm with a little girl called Diana. She was not a very friendly pigeon. She made fun of all the animals and Diana was very worried about all the trouble she was causing.

One day, Diana's friend Lisa brought her another pigeon. His name was Brutus and he was very strong. He charged at Polly and then retreated hastily inside his pigeon-house. Polly was quite badly hurt and Diana looked after her carefully.

When winter came, the pigeon was still lame and she kept slipping on the ice. The hens teased poor Polly just as she had teased them. But the rabbits made two little skis out of wood for her, so that she could ski anywhere she liked.

Polly was a happy pigeon now and she was friendly to everyone.

 **342**

Peter and Paul

Peter and Paul were twins. Each Saturday morning they took it in turns to visit an old lady down the road, but the old lady could never tell the twins apart.

On their birthday, the twins invited the old lady to tea. When she arrived, she handed Peter and Paul two bright woollen scarves, with their names embroidered on the ends.

'Now I shall know you, when you come visiting again,' she laughed.

343

A Very Unusual Owl

'It snowed during the night,' said Josie to her friend the owl. 'Come on, let's go skiing!'

The owl perched on Josie's shoulder and they went outside.

'Put on your skis,' said Josie to her friend.

The owl's skis were two planks of wood. He put a stock under each wing and he was ready.

'Off we go!' cried Josie . . . and they flew down the snowy slope.

'Oh, my goodness,' thought the owl, 'I'm going much too fast. Ooh . . . !'

Then, over he went! He dropped his stocks and went sliding head-first into a tree trunk. He felt very sore.

'Nothing broken, that's lucky.'

'What a champion skier!' exclaimed Josie. 'Well done! But where are your stocks?'

'I don't need them,' replied the owl. 'I've had enough skiing for today!'

344

Honey

Who makes honey for my tea?
I make honey, said the bee.
Where do you find it, Mr Bee?
I suck it from the flowers, you see.
Do you have jam-jars in your home?
No, I just use a honeycomb.
What happens when you've saved a lot?
The beeman puts it in a pot!

✳ 345

Joseph Goes to the Zoo

One Sunday, Joseph and his Grandmother went to the zoo to see all the animals.

Joseph liked the monkeys best and by lunch-time they had walked as far as their cage. Joseph gave them some peanuts, which they gobbled up hungrily. He was having such a good time that he did not notice that his Grandmother had disappeared.

Being a sensible little boy, he decided to wait by the cage until the keeper came along. He was just thinking how hungry he was, when the monkeys gave him some of their bananas. They were delicious.

At last, the keeper arrived and found his Grandmother. Before they went home, Joseph said goodbye and thank you to all his friends the monkeys.

✳ 346

Cheeky the Mouse

Cheeky, the little mouse, was always poking her nose into things. 'Mmm, that cheese smells good,' she said.

'Just watch out for the cat,' warned her Mother one day.

So, Cheeky tiptoed very quietly towards the pantry . . . she liked it in there. Suddenly . . . crash! . . . she had tipped over a pot of honey. The cat pounced and Cheeky ran squeaking all the way back to her hole.

347 Summertime

Summer's the play-by-the-stream time;
Roll-in-the-meadow-and-dream time,
Lie-on-your-back-and-chew-grass time,
Watch-butterflies-as-they-pass time,
Try-and-pick-daisies-with-toes time,
Playing-where-nobody-knows time.

348 Moses' Toeses

Moses supposes his toeses are roses,
But Moses supposes erroneously;
For nobody's toeses are posies of roses
As Moses supposes his toeses to be.

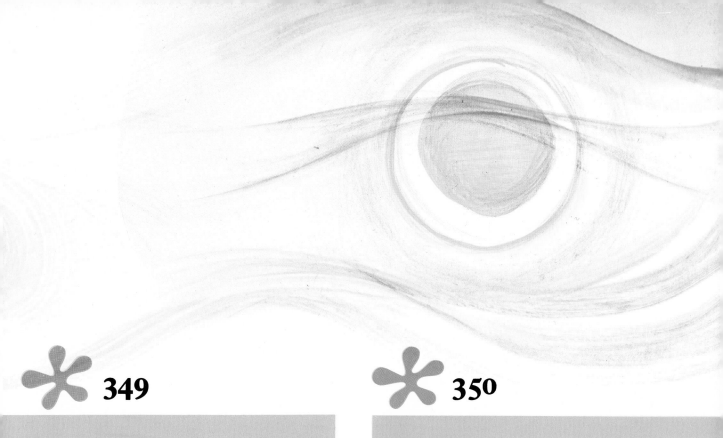

349

Sneezes

Sneeze on Monday, sneeze for danger ;
Sneeze on Tuesday, kiss a stranger ;
Sneeze on Wednesday, sneeze for a letter ;
Sneeze on Thursday, something better ;
Sneeze on Friday, sneeze for sorrow ;
Sneeze on Saturday, joy for tomorrow.

350

Sally

Sally go round the sun,
Sally go round the moon,
Sally go round the chimney-pots
On a Saturday afternoon.

351

Where's Catherine?

'Come on,' said Mummy, 'we've finished all our shopping now, so let's go home.'

'Good!' said Daddy. 'Everyone into the car.' All the children bundled into the car, and off they went. When they got home, Daddy took the shopping out of the car and the boys carried it inside.

Annie ran off with her ball.

'Cathy, Cathy, where are you?'

'Mummy, where are you? Is Cathy there too?'

'Daddy, is Cathy with you?'

'Wasn't she in the car?' asked Daddy.

'Oh dear,' cried Annie, 'we've lost Cathy.'

'We must have left her in town.'

Daddy and Mummy drove back to find her. There was Cathy standing on the pavement. She had tear stains on her cheeks and she was holding a packet of sweets that a kind lady had given her.

'Oh Cathy, you are lucky,' said Annie. 'Next time I'll be lost too!'

352

Tom Comes Home

Everybody was very upset. Patrick's little dog Tom, who used to go with Patrick everywhere had got lost on their last walk in the forest. The silly little fellow had gone racing after a young rabbit and had lost his way.

As evening fell, Patrick had to abandon his search and go home, all alone. For days afterwards, Patrick and his family looked everywhere for Tom, but they could not find him.

As the days passed, it grew colder and colder, and Patrick tossed and turned in bed at night, worrying about his little dog.

Then, one morning, Patrick heard a scratching noise at the door. It was Tom, all ragged and thin, and trembling with cold. He threw himself happily into his master's arms.

Now whenever Tom goes chasing rabbits he makes sure Patrick is not far behind.

Busy Children

'Ssh, children,' said Daddy, 'Mother has a cold. Be good now.'

'Yes Daddy, we will.'

Sam got busy washing the dishes, and sang a little song as he worked.

'You'll wake Mummy,' said Caroline.

Don, the youngest of the children, was in his bath, playing with his toy ducks.

'Mummy's awake,' announced Sam. 'Let's make her some tea.' When it was ready Don and Sam carried the tea-tray and Caroline followed them with a rose that she had picked from the garden.

'This will make you feel better, Mummy,' they said.

'Oh, I've spilt the tea in your saucer,' sighed Caroline.

'And I'm afraid your toast is a little burnt,' said Patrick.

'Mmm,' said Father as he came in, 'you've got something nice to eat.'

'I'm feeling much better,' said Mother. 'The children have been looking after me.'

'Of course,' said the children, 'we're very good cooks.'

354

Lazy Frances

Frances was a lazy little girl.

One morning, her Mummy asked her to help make the breakfast.

Frances replied wearily, 'I don't want to,' and sat down on a chair.

Suddenly, a very strange thing happened. She was looking at her reflection in the window, when she saw the letters of her name taking shape on the glass. They twisted themselves around until they made the shape of a horrid old hag.

'That's not me, is it?' thought Frances.

'Oh Mummy,' she said quickly, 'I didn't mean it – I will help you.'

Before she started work, she looked once more in the window. The letters had become pretty birds and butterflies. The birds twittered happily to her and Mummy wondered why Frances was smiling.

355

I Had a Little Pony

I had a little pony,
His name was Dapple Grey;
I lent him to a lady
To ride a mile away.

She whipped him, she slashed him,
She rode him through the mire;
I would not lend my pony now
For all the lady's hire.

Little Brother

'Helena, I want to tell you a secret.'

'What is it, Mummy?'

'Soon you will have a little brother or sister,' said Mummy, smiling.

'Oh, how lovely,' said Helena excitedly. 'But, when will he be here?'

'In a few months,' replied Mummy.

'That's a long time,' cried Helena as she ran off to tell all her friends.

The months seemed like years to Helena, but she was kept busy helping Mummy. Then, one afternoon, Daddy said, 'Come and see your little brother.' Helena crept up to the bassinet and looked in.

'Oh, he's just like a doll!' she cried. Then, she hugged her parents, exclaiming, 'He's beautiful, and he's my very own brother!'

356

My Sweets

Mummy is shopping,
I'm all by myself,
My favourite toffees
Are here on this shelf.
I'm reaching on tip-toes,
I've got them, I'm sure . . .
Oh, dear me! I've dropped them,
Down on the floor!

358

Alexander's Christmas Tree

Alexander's Father was a woodcutter. It was three days before Christmas, and he was going into the forest to cut down a fir tree. Alexander went with him and two rabbits followed on behind. Rufus Fox and Red Squirrel met them on the way.

Alexander's Father chose a fine, sturdy fir tree, then he cut through its trunk with a saw.

Three sparrows came and stood in front of Alexander. 'Tweet, tweet! What's happening?'

'It will be Christmas soon and I'm going to decorate this little tree. And, I would like you all to come round to my house on Christmas day.'

At Christmas, the fir tree sparkled in the living room, with all its lights and tinsel. The animals from the forest arrived carrying presents – Squirrel brought acorns and walnuts, and the two rabbits brought a shiny coin that they had found lying on the ground.

The fire crackled, the birds sang merrily and everyone had a wonderful time.

'Happy Christmas,' said Alexander to all his friends.

228

A Special Treat

Timber Tim was a lumberjack's cat. He lived in a log cabin near a lake in the middle of a pine forest.

Timber Tim had two special friends – the bear cubs. While his master was at work in the forest. Timber Tim would play rough and tumble with them or they would sit by the lake and try to catch fish with the ducklings.

At Christmas time the lumberjacks brought little fir trees home to their log cabins.

On Christmas Eve, Timber Tim's master decorated his tree with sparkling lights and pretty things. Timber Tim thought it looked beautiful. Then Timber Tim's master put it outside! 'How strange,' thought Timber Tim.

On Christmas morning, Timber Tim had a wonderful surprise. There, in the garden his friends the bear cubs and one of the ducklings were gathered round the Christmas tree. Timber Tim's kind master had caught a dish full of delicious fish for them as a special Christmas treat.

'Christmas isn't the same unless you share it with some friends,' said Timber Tim's master.

And Timber Tim rang the log cabin bell for joy!

Ginger's Christmas

Ginger the cat was very unhappy. It would soon be Christmas and all his friends on the farm were talking about the presents they were going to receive and the beautiful Christmas tree that they would have.

Ginger did not have any family. He knew that he would not be given any presents and that he would not have a Christmas tree, and his friends weren't likely to remember him. On Christmas Eve, he would go into the barn to sleep. It would be cold and he would be all alone, and he would cry. It was not much fun being an orphan, and not having any brothers or sisters to play with, or a Mother and Father to tell him stories.

When Christmas Eve arrived, all the farm animals were busy carrying presents here and there. Some of them were hauling the Christmas tree inside. Ginger watched them from the shadows and as night fell, he crept into the barn and stretched out on the straw. He could not sleep because there was too much noise all around him, with everyone laughing and singing.

Suddenly, Ginger heard a scratching at the door. He got up and went to open it. It was Turkey in his finest suit. Ginger followed him into a big shed. All the farm animals were gathered there and when Ginger came in, they all began to sing, 'Happy Christmas, Ginger.'

The little cat could not believe his eyes and he thought he was dreaming. In front of him there stood a huge fir tree, all lit up, with real stars that had come down from the sky especially for him and the moon perched on top. On each branch there were presents, and there were bright streamers everywhere.

To one side, on a big table covered in a white cloth, there were plates piled high with chocolates and other sweets waiting to be eaten.

One after the other, the farm animals all came up to Ginger and gave him presents.

As he had thought he would, Ginger

230

cried, but this time for joy. He did not know how to thank his friends. But when they asked him to sing a song, he did so in his best voice, accompanied on the accordion by Porker the pig, on the flute by Rabbit and on the guitar by Cecil, the horse. Everyone in the audience clapped and the party went on all through the night.

Ginger knew he would remember that Christmas Eve for a long time to come.

 361
Paul and Grandmamma

Grandmamma seemed upset. Paul had not been very good while his parents were away. He had broken one of her best plates, left his toys all over the house, smothered himself in jam as he ate his toast and dirtied his new clothes.

'Would you like me to sweep the snow off the garden path?' asked Paul, who felt very sorry for all he had done and wanted to make her feel happy again.

Grandmamma cried, 'Well, well. You're not such a bad little rascal after all!' and her face broke into a big smile.

 362
Nicky, Where Are You?

Nicky belonged to Mary. He was a friendly little dog.

One morning, he ran off and Mary went looking for him.

'Nicky, Nicky, where are you?' Then she began to cry. She thought she would never find him.

'Woof, woof,' barked Nicky as he scampered up. 'It's your birthday Mary, and I went to get you a bunch of roses.'

363

Henry Goes to School

Mother and Father Rabbit had a baby bunny called Henry. He was their only son.

One day, when he was still quite small, he said, 'I would like to go to school today.' So, he packed a bag with his lunch and set off. Mother and Father Rabbit were too shocked to say anything and as their little son hopped off down the road, Mother Rabbit burst into tears, saying, 'But he's so young. Anything could happen to him.'

But that afternoon, Henry came hopping home with lots of other bunnies. 'I had such a lovely day at school,' he said to his parents, 'and these are all my new friends.'

364

Ragamuffin

'Ragamuffin, it's time to go to the party. You can take off that old dress now and put on your new one.'

Ragamuffin did as her Mother said and pulled on her new dress. Then she ran downstairs and drank her hot chocolate.

'Oh no,' cried her Mother, as Ragamuffin spilt the chocolate down the front of her dress. 'We'll never be able to wash that off. Now you'll just have to wear your old dress to the party!'

365

Bad-tempered Sally-Anne

Sally-Anne was always in a temper. As soon as the alarm clock went off in the morning, she would throw it down on the floor crying angrily, 'That's enough! Be quiet . . . let me sleep.'

When she took a dress out of her wardrobe, she always grumbled, 'Pooh, all these dresses are horrible.'

She treated all her toys badly.

Often, she pushed away her cup of milk so roughly that the cup fell over and chipped, and the milk went all over the floor. In fact, Sally-Anne was so unpleasant that all the things in her room decided to teach her a lesson.

The next morning the alarm clock deliberately forgot to ring and Sally-Anne got up so late that Mother was very cross. Then, for fear of being knocked over, the milk cup hid in the cupboard, so that Sally-Anne had to go without breakfast. Her dresses all fell in a crumpled heap, leaving Sally-Anne with nothing to wear. Her dolls and toys ran away to the children next-door.

'I'm hungry . . . I'm cold . . . and I'm bored!' moaned Sally-Anne. But no-one came to comfort her.

Sally-Anne had learnt her lesson and the next day she was so nice that her alarm clock began to ring again, her dresses climbed back on their hangers, her milk cup, her dolls and her toys all came back, and everyone was happy.

366

Alice Celebrates New Year

It was New Year's Eve and Alice was all alone in her house at the end of the village. She did not have any family or friends.

She had made herself some supper, but she did not really want to eat it because she felt so sad at being all on her own.

Suddenly, she heard a sound outside. Who could be coming to see her on this, the last day of the year?

She opened the door and saw a big dog sitting in the street as if he were waiting for something. His fur was shaggy and he looked at her with friendly eyes as if to say, 'My master has left me and I am alone too. If you like, we could spend New Year's Eve together.'

'You have come at just the right time Mr Dog. You can keep me company and share my supper,' said Alice, who was delighted.

Mr Dog wagged his tail with pleasure. Supper was just what he needed.

And so Alice and Mr Dog sat down together and ate their supper and celebrated the coming of the New Year.

235

Stories in this book

1 2 3 4 5 6 7 9 10 11

23 25 47 46

24 33 34

45 140 32 81

263 269 152 291

225 235 178

150 156 181

268

290 247 302 307

350 343 351